"I don't go to hotels with men. Even if I used to know them."

All the sadness she felt came out in her tone. He used to know that about her. She didn't know the Garrett he'd become.

"That's not what I meant." Garrett sighed. "You're safe with me. You know that. Or you should. The party scene got old a year ago."

Her heart clenched. Had he really changed his ways? Was this Garrett closer to the one she used to know?

"I want someone who cares about me." Garrett squeezed her hand. "Not for my fame or money, but for me."

And he was looking straight at that someone.

"A friend, that's all I'm looking for. The road gets long and lonely. I could use somebody to touch base with, maybe call every once in a while. To keep me grounded. You were always great at that." Loneliness echoed in his voice. "Say yes."

Books by Shannon Taylor Vannatter

Love Inspired Heartsong Presents

Rodeo Regrets
Rodeo Queen
Rodeo Song

SHANNON TAYLOR VANNATTER

is a stay-at-home mom and pastor's wife. Her debut novel won a 2011 Inspirational Readers' Choice Award. When not writing, she runs circles in the care and feeding of her husband, their son and their church congregation. Home is a central Arkansas zoo with two charcoal-gray cats, a chocolate Lab and three dachshunds in weenie-dog heaven. If given the chance to clean house or write, she'd rather write. Her goal is to hire Alice from *The Brady Bunch*.

SHANNON TAYLOR VANNATTER

Rodeo Song

HEARTSONG
PRESENTS

Recycling programs
for this product may
not exist in your area.

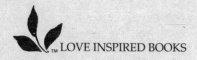 ™ LOVE INSPIRED BOOKS

ISBN-13: 978-0-373-48706-6

RODEO SONG

www.Harlequin.com

Printed in U.S.A.

"Delight thyself also in the Lord;
and he shall give thee the desires of thine heart."
—*Psalms* 37:4

I dedicate this book to my husband
for not minding if I dream about cowboys all day.

Acknowledgments

I appreciate DeeDee Barker-Wix, Director of Sales
at the Cowtown Coliseum, Julia Buswold,
Executive Director Texas Cowboy Hall of Fame,
Katherine M. Kolstad with Billy Bob's Texas,
Aubrey Librarian, Kathy Ramsey, Judy Cochran with
the Ever After Chapel, and Steve and Krys Murray,
owners of Moms on Main.

Chapter 1

Screaming fans surrounded Jenna Wentworth as Garrett Steele's rich, seductive voice and acoustic guitar drove the enraptured women into a frenzy. And despite her painful past with him, his lush baritone melted her insides.

Thirtieth row, floor seating. Jenna peered through the chaos, but with everyone standing, she couldn't see much onstage. Her first country-music concert. Ever. Stale beer assaulted her senses and her ears would probably ring for a week. Why had she come?

Because her friend Tori had promised to attend church with her in return, but…that wasn't the whole story.

Truth be told—she couldn't resist getting a glimpse of Garrett again. Pathetic.

The music stopped. Applause, whistles and screams shattered her eardrums.

"What an awesome crowd." Garrett's words boomed over the speakers. "We're taking a short break but we'll be back, so don't go anywhere, Dallas."

The crowd roared and the lights brightened. She stood on her tiptoes long enough to peer around the tall man standing in front of her to get a fleeting glimpse of Garrett leaving the stage before it went dark.

"I can't believe I'm here," Tori shouted over the clamor. "He's even better looking in person."

Jenna's mouth went dry as the arena lights brightened. "How can you tell what he looks like?"

Maybe his floozy, boozy lifestyle had taken its toll, but Jenna couldn't tell from the few glimpses she'd gotten of him.

"He's just the greatest." Tori did a little bounce.

Sure. Jenna rolled her eyes. The greatest guy to ever walk out on her.

"Okay, Jenna, I know you don't really like him, but can't you humor me?"

Time for a distraction. "I'm thirsty. Let's get something to drink."

They inched slowly up the stands toward the lobby, along with half the crowd in the American Airlines Center.

She could happily not talk about Garrett—if only she could stop thinking about him, too.

Tori would be beside herself if she knew Jenna had grown up with him. That she'd once had feelings for him much deeper than *like*. Had once been the girl he'd claimed to love.

Though the cold bite of New Year's Day lurked outside, the lobby was toasty warm. But the line at the concession stand was endless. At this rate, they'd never get anything to drink.

Among the crowd of adoring fans, dutiful husbands and shrewd boyfriends, Jenna blended in like a Queen Anne wingback in a farmhouse.

Several amorous couples surrounded them. Men obviously brought their dates to Garrett Steele concerts to perform the dance of seduction for them. And it was working. All too well. Jenna closed her eyes.

Past simply thirsty, her tongue stuck to the roof of her mouth.

"Look! It's Garrett Steele!" Excited voices echoed through the lobby.

In the distance, security guards cleared a path. Garrett ran toward the concession stand pursued by a trail of women.

Tori and a herd of females surged toward him. Men, deserted by their dates, stood as if rooted to the spot. Jenna moved closer to the counter to avoid the mob. Surreal. At least she'd get her tea faster now.

Though the women ran to meet Garrett head-on, they ended up in the throng behind him with the security guards keeping them at bay. Hands grabbed and clawed at Garrett as he and his entourage got closer to her. She could no longer see Tori. The rush forced abandoned men to move out of the way.

Please don't see me. Please don't see me. Please don't see me. The pathetic one he'd turned his back on—at his concert with the rest of his minions.

Brilliant green eyes locked with hers. A flick of recognition followed by a familiar grin. Her heart went into overdrive. Surely she'd swoon. Mere feet away from her now, he held his hand out toward her. As if of their own volition, her fingers clasped his as he ran past, dragging her with him.

What was she doing? Hadn't she been sucked in by him once before? And in exchange for her brainless devotion, she'd gotten her heart broken.

Jenna fought to keep up with Garrett's pace. Too late to turn back now, the stampede behind them encouraged speed despite her strappy heels.

He slowed only when they squeezed through a doorway and descended the stairs back into the sunken arena, then surged toward a smaller platform at the other end from the main stage. Security guards surrounded them as Garrett guided her up the steps. A guard tried to pull her hand from his.

"No!" he shouted above the chaos. "I want her onstage with me."

Her stomach did a flip-flop. "No!"

The pandemonium surrounding them carried her protest away and the guard helped her up the stairs.

"It's okay. I won't force you to sing." Garrett winked. "Even though you have a lovely voice."

Her heart pooled at his feet, but her insides twisted in knots as he led her to a tall stool. Weak-kneed, she gratefully perched on it. His band and backup singers faded to the back of the stage. A spotlight blinded her.

The music started—the opening notes of his signature wedding song—"One Day." She'd heard it countless times over the past month with his voice crooning to her at Walmart, restaurants and the streets of the Fort Worth Stockyards historic district as Texas proudly gave its star plenty of airtime.

Until finally, she'd downloaded it on her iPod. A few times, she'd allowed herself the guilty pleasure of listening. Okay, more than a few times.

Pathetic. She inwardly cringed.

His green gaze imprisoned hers as he sang the words of adoration.

Years of searching finally over,
just when I'd given up on love.
You're my lucky four-leaf clover,
only sent from up above.

Desperate to tune out his serenade of undying love for her, she picked a spot on a speaker to stare at. But her gaze returned to him as if pulled by a magnet.

His dark, wavy hair hung way past his shoulders. Nothing like the short mop-top he'd worn in school. She didn't usually like long hair on men, but the flowing waves and olive skin were the perfect contrast for his grass-green eyes and framed his high cheekbones, chiseled bone structure and scruffy-beard-shadowed jaw—male-model material.

His honky-tonk years hadn't hurt his looks a bit. Only God could put something so breathtaking together.

When the instrumental part of the song began, he knelt at her feet—as if to propose. The proposal she'd dreamed of. The proposal that had never come. Her heart took a nosedive.

Since middle school, Garrett had had one goal in mind—stardom. And in the end, it hadn't included her.

Yet Jenna remembered him in the church choir. Okay, she'd joined the choir just to be close to him. Yep—pathetic.

Despite the intense heat given off by the lights above, she shuddered. It wasn't because of his proximity. No, she was so over him. She was just nervous. Onstage in front of thousands of people.

The music swelled and his baritone tugged at her.

Can't believe I finally found you,
I looked for you all of my life.
I don't know what I did without you,
but I know one day you'll be my wife.

As he mesmerized the audience, making her the envy of every woman there, she resisted the urge to clamp her hands over her ears and block him out. Okay, she wasn't over him. And probably never would be. She'd die an old maid still in love with Garrett Steele.

The song ended. He stood and kissed her hand as the lights brightened.

Her hand tingled and warmth swept up her arms. She could still feel the strength of his arms, the tenderness of his kiss as if it were yesterday.

"Ladies and gentlemen, this is Jenna Wentworth. Jenna and I grew up together, so when I saw her in the lobby, I couldn't resist staging a little impromptu reunion. Give Jenna a big hand for being such a good sport."

The crowd erupted. With the glare of hot lights, she couldn't see a thing, and sweat trickled down the hollow of her back.

Garrett took her hand and led her to the steps. He shot her a wink and handed her over to a security guard. Dismissed.

The security man led her off the stage. Her heel caught on the step, but he steadied her. "I'll escort you back to your seat."

"Thank you, but that's not necessary. I'm going back to the concession stand." Her legs wobbled; her pulse hammered. Jenna climbed the stairs up to the lobby with as much nonchalance as she could muster. Thank goodness for the handrail.

"Even more beautiful than I remember. Oh…" Regret sounded in Garrett's voice. "I forgot to get her number. Sebastian, get her number for me."

Heat crept up her neck.

Whistles, catcalls and laughter rippled through the crowd.

"Not like that." Garrett's sigh huffed in the microphone. "Just to keep in touch."

Just walk. Ignore him. He's only putting on a good show. Toying with her. *Get through the rest of the concert. Go home and back to normal.* Leave him behind just as he'd left her eight years ago.

Finally up the endless stairs, she walked to the lineless concession stand and ordered her long-awaited large tea. The cool liquid bathed her parched throat as she trudged back to the arena. At least she'd gotten her exercise for the day. If only she could talk Tori into leaving—now.

She'd had enough of memory lane. She'd wanted a glimpse of Garrett. Not a close-up. Great! Now his eyes would haunt her dreams. Again.

As Garrett sang another love song back on the main stage, Jenna climbed over feet and purses to her seat.

Tori grabbed her arm and jumped up and down. Her mouth moved, but Jenna couldn't hear a word. Surely the concert couldn't last much longer.

The rest of the love songs blurred in Jenna's mind. Garrett finally closed the last song and left the stage. But, as the cheers resonated through the building, he reentered and stepped onto center stage.

"What a great crowd. Thanks, Dallas. It's great to be home, and thanks, Jenna, for—" his voice caught "—letting me bask in your beauty."

Heat seared her cheeks.

The drummer counted a beat and the band struck up again for Garrett's encore.

As the final notes faded away, the stage went black to thunderous applause. The arena lights came on, the crowd began to quiet and the two friends inched into the slow-moving throng toward the lobby.

"I can't believe you know Garrett Steele." Tori whacked her on the arm. "Why didn't you tell me?"

"Would you have believed me?"

"You know him and got to go onstage with him. You don't even like him. That's so unfair!" Tori wailed.

Jenna shrugged. "He wasn't Garrett the country star when we had chemistry together." In more ways than one.

"Garrett Steele." Tori grabbed Jenna by both shoulders and shook her lightly. "*The Garrett Steele* just sang a love song to you! He kissed your hand! You can never wash that hand again. How can you stay so calm?"

Calm. She could still feel the touch of his lips on her hand. Her quivering insides were anything but calm. A long time ago, he'd kissed her lips—on more than one occasion.

Several other women in the crowd recognized her and gathered around her as if she were an exhibit. A few even asked for her autograph. She made it to the lobby, without signing anything, and headed for the refuge of the bathroom.

A large muscular man stepped into her path with the word *Security* emblazoned in gold letters across the front of his black T-shirt.

"I'm Sebastian. Mr. Steele would like to see you backstage, Miss Wentworth. Follow me, please."

How dare Garrett summon her. Did he really expect her to do his bidding? To show up all moony-eyed over him?

Why wouldn't he? She'd practically drooled onstage. Oh, why couldn't she get over him?

"Jenna?" Tori's finger dug into her ribs.

"Umm." Jenna swallowed hard. "I think he was just kidding."

Sebastian's eyes widened.

Probably no other woman on the premises would question the request. Several concertgoers shot her curious glances on their way to the exit.

"Mr. Steele never jokes about such things. He told me to find you and bring you back."

She sucked in a deep breath. Just how many women did Sebastian retrieve each year for Garrett? She knew all about Garrett's reputation and exploits. How could he have turned his back on Jesus? On her?

Her heart tensed. So she wasn't over him, but maybe she could remind him of where he came from. And how far he'd strayed. But at the risk of losing her heart to him again?

"I really need to head home." She pulled off an indifferent shrug. "It'll take forever just to get out of the parking lot, and we've got an hour drive ahead of us."

"Mr. Steele simply needs a few minutes of your time to thank you for your cooperation. In the meantime, the parking lot will clear. And if it's still congested when you're ready to leave, I can get you out."

"Are you crazy?" Tori tugged at her arm. "He wants you backstage. Garrett Steele wants to see you backstage. Don't blow it. Go!"

Despite everything, she did want to see him. And if Jenna got Tori an introduction to Garrett, maybe she'd come to church more than just once.

"Can my friend come, too?"

"Sure." Sebastian nodded. "Follow me."

Tori let out a whoop.

Maybe God did have a plan in all of this.

"You know I wouldn't do this for just anyone," Jenna whispered as they followed the guard. "You owe me big, and we can't stay long, just a couple of minutes."

"I can't believe this!" Tori giggled almost hysterically. "I'll never forget this night as long as I live!"

Jenna rolled her eyes.

They followed Sebastian down a long hallway lined by expectant-looking fans. Were these people waiting for the band to walk through? Sebastian opened a door and ushered them inside a large, sparsely furnished room.

Garrett stood in the middle of a small crowd, but when he saw her, he rushed toward her with a hug.

Why did his arms have to feel just as good as they had eight years ago? She pulled away before she could get too used to his embrace.

"This is my friend Tori Eaton." She swallowed the boulder in her throat. "She wanted to meet you."

"Nice to meet you." Garrett's gaze never left Jenna's face. "I just wanted to thank you for going along with me out there."

Please don't ask me why I did.

"We always do the lobby run, but I've never taken anyone onstage." He took her hand, and his touch shot fireworks through her veins. "I saw you and just went with it. I think it added to the concert." He winked at her. "Maybe you should travel with me and we could make it part of the act."

Steam would surely blow out her ears any minute. So he had used her. She was only part of his act.

"I don't think so." At least she sounded calm. She looked past Garrett and tried to catch Tori's eye. Her friend, busy getting autographs and visiting with the band, was completely oblivious to Jenna.

"You're not in a relationship, are you? I mean—I don't want to worry about some irate boyfriend."

"Nothing to worry about there." The only man she'd ever wanted a relationship with was him.

"Then why couldn't you travel with me?" He shot her a wicked grin.

Her blood flared again. She could handle a lot of things, but not Garrett's teasing. "Because I love my home in Aubrey, and my mother would be horrified if I took up country music. No offense."

"Probably as horrified as mine was."

His parents. Such wonderful people. He should be ashamed for all the embarrassment he'd caused them. But apparently he had no shame. "I run into your parents every once in a while. How are they?"

"Enjoying travel. I finally convinced them to let me bankroll their early retirement." He winced. "It was the least I could do for all the hurt I've put them through."

Maybe he did have shame.

"It's good to see you, Jenna." His knuckles lightly grazed her cheek.

The sound of her name on his lips numbed her brain as his touch ignited flames across her skin. Double whammy. She shivered. *He's only a man,* she reminded herself. A very promiscuous man.

"I knew you hadn't changed a bit when I saw you standing there in the lobby."

Concentrate on his words instead of the tingling cheek. Maybe she hadn't changed, but he had.

"This thunderous storm swarmed around me and there you stood, so calm, the eye in the middle of my hurricane." Seduction laced his voice. "Have dinner with me?"

He'd probably used a similar line on countless other females. Yet his charm tempted her to do whatever he wanted. Had Eve's serpent sounded like Garrett Steele?

She took a step back. "I can't. We need to go. It's late."

"Wait." He gently caught her arm. "You own some kind of business, don't you?"

"Worthwhile Designs, an interior-decorating boutique." He'd never understood her dream. She sighed.

A genuine smile made his eyes shimmer. "That's awesome. You achieved your dream."

Not exactly. She'd dreamed of a store at the upscale mall Galleria Dallas. Instead, she sold custom designed horseshoe-embellished curtain rods and wagon-wheel light fixtures. And she'd dreamed of being married to Garrett.

But Fort Worth had been good to her. "And you achieved yours."

"Somewhat." He shrugged. "So do you actually do the designing?"

"Yes. Tori and I met at design school and she works for me." Jenna peered around him for Tori, but her friend had disappeared.

"Do you work on Saturday?"

"No." Where had Tori gone? Her stomach twisted. They needed to leave. She needed to get away from Garrett and his beckoning green eyes.

"Then you don't need to rush off, since you don't work tomorrow." Garrett smiled.

Oh, yes, she did need to rush off. She scanned the room. "Where's Tori?" Her voice came out tight.

He frowned and turned away. "Andy, where did the other girl go?"

"Rick invited her to the party with the band."

"What?" Tori had left without her?

"There's always a party after the concert. I guess my band invited your friend. It's at the Hyatt. Would you like to go?"

"The only place I want to go is home." Desperation sounded in her tone.

The door opened. *Let it be Tori.*

A woman entered. She exuded elegance. Flawless skin, sleek blond hair topped with a red cowgirl hat tipped just so. The red blingy dress hugged all the right curves and revealed long legs. Even with the stilettos, she still stood on tiptoe to kiss Sebastian.

Jenna's gaze darted away from the private moment.

"Listen, I usually skip the party anyway. Join me for dinner? I have a suite. We can order room service, and one of my boys can bring your friend back in an hour or so."

"I'm not going to your suite." She propped her hands on both hips. "Please get one of your boys to bring Tori back now."

"Hey, it's me, Garrett. Have I ever tried anything with you?"

Only sweet kisses. Her cheeks warmed. But that was before all his groupies and supermodels.

"Just give me an hour. We can catch up." He took her hand. "Look, your friend is having the time of her life, and she'd never forgive you if you ruined it for her."

Her heart pounded harder than the bass drum in Garrett's band. Tori was a black belt. She could take care of herself. She probably did this sort of thing often. *Mental note—never go anywhere with Tori outside of work again.*

"I'm not like Tori. I don't go to hotels with men. Even if I used to know them." All the sadness she felt came out in her tone. He used to know that about her. She didn't know the Garrett he'd become.

"That's not what I meant." Garrett sighed. "You're safe with me. You know that. Or you should. The party scene got old a year ago."

Her heart tightened. Had he really changed his ways? Was this Garrett closer to the one she used to know?

"I want someone who cares about me." Garrett squeezed her hand. "Not for my fame or money, but for me."

And he was looking straight at that someone.

"A friend, that's all I'm looking for. The road gets long and lonely. I could use somebody to touch base with, maybe call every once in a while. To keep me grounded. You were always great at that." Loneliness echoed in his voice. "Say yes."

Jenna couldn't form the words, and worse, she didn't know what she'd say if she could.

Chapter 2

Garrett's throat constricted. "An hour, Jenna. That's all I'm asking." An hour to rediscover the woman he'd never stopped loving.

Indecision played over her features.

Garrett longed to kiss her, but she didn't trust him anymore. Why should she after all she'd probably heard about him in the news over the years they'd been apart?

"Why not go to a restaurant instead of your hotel?" She nibbled her lip.

"It's midnight and I don't get to go out in public like the rest of the world." He sighed and pushed his hair away from his face. "That would be chaos. And besides, I want to have a quiet dinner. We'll dine in one of the meeting rooms. Sebastian and his wife, Amanda, always join me for dinner since they don't do the party scene, either."

Jenna's gaze swung back to Amanda. She stood with her back against Sebastian and his arms around her waist.

"They're crazy about each other." Garrett heard the longing in his tone. Did she? "She's one of my backup singers and they've both toured with me for seven years."

"I'd rather go home."

What was so bad about the thought of spending an hour with him? "If you're determined to wait on your friend, what else are you going to do?"

Her shoulders slumped. "Okay."

"You don't have to sound so excited about it." He grinned, trying not to let his hurt show. "My chauffeur is waiting."

"I'd rather take my car."

"I thought you trusted me."

"I don't want any of your employees or the hotel staff thinking I'm some groupie." Her face bloomed pink.

Ouch. "Are you always this stubborn?"

"Yes."

"I was hoping you'd grown out of it." The exact stubbornness that had made her refuse to go on the road with him all those years ago. He handed her a business card. "Here's my contact info. Guard it with your life. Do you have a card? I can give it to my security detail so you don't run into any problems at the hotel."

Obediently, she dug a card from her purse and gave it to him. "I'll be fine."

He grabbed her hand. "I will see you there, won't I? You won't stand me up?" No woman had ever stood him up. But he wouldn't put it past this one. And this was the only one who mattered.

Had any woman ever stood up Garrett Steele? She doubted it.

"I'm not the one who walks out on people." She deliberately infused bitterness into her tone to hide the hurt.

Garrett winced. "I asked you to come with me, Jenna."

Yes, but he hadn't been willing to stay for her. As soon as they'd graduated, he'd bolted—in hot pursuit of his dream. Leaving her behind. "Did you really think I could have run a decorating business from the road?"

"I figured you could start up in Nashville, and then once my career took flight, you could let someone else run it."

"But I wanted my business in Texas. And I didn't want to let someone else run it." A frustrated sigh escaped. "I wanted the business, but I wanted to be a decorator, too."

"I guess I never thought about that."

"Exactly." He'd expected her to drop her dream and follow his. But had she expected him to do the same? Or compromise and live in Aubrey, fly back and forth to Nashville, and never tour? With that plan, his career would never have found wings. But maybe he wouldn't have lost himself.

"That's all ancient history." She waved an unconcerned hand through the air. "We're both happily living our dreams." Apart. Maybe not so happily. On her end, anyway.

Movement beside them caught her attention. Sebastian. "Sorry to interrupt, boss, but I'm taking my little lady back to the hotel."

Garrett took Jenna's hand in his and her pulse rocketed. "Jenna Wentworth, you've already met Sebastian Smythe. This is his wife, Amanda."

"Your part in the show tonight was great." Amanda playfully punched Garrett on the shoulder. "I couldn't believe it when you came dragging her up to the stage."

"Just keeping things interesting." Garrett shrugged. "Sebastian, can you see Jenna to her car? She's agreed to join us for dinner in one of the private meeting rooms at the hotel tonight."

"Sure." Sebastian frowned and opened the door for her. "This way, Miss Wentworth."

But as Jenna exited, a woman burst through. Jet-black hair, red lips, slinky dress. The woman's gaze locked on Garrett.

"Desiree, what are you doing here?" Shock and discomfort filled Garrett's tone.

So he knew the woman.

"I've been trying to reach you." Seduction laced the woman's voice.

Who was she? A girlfriend? A groupie?

"Excuse me." Jenna sidestepped the woman.

"I'll see you in about twenty minutes," Garrett called after her.

Sebastian shuffled her through the waiting crowd and out into the evening air.

"I'm three blocks away. You don't have to take me to my car."

"Three blocks is no problem. I'd like to ask you something anyway. Are you a Christian?"

She blinked. This night kept getting weirder. "Yes. Why do you ask?"

"I overheard part of your conversation backstage with Garrett. Most women fall at his feet. My wife and I are Christians. We've been trying to witness to him for years but can't seem to get anywhere."

Her insides quivered. Garrett was a Christian, too. But he'd forgotten.

"He needs someone like you in his life, to keep him focused."

"Until tonight, I hadn't seen him in years." Her heart hitched. She gulped the fresh chill of January evening air.

At least the crowd was gone. No one stalked her for her autograph as they neared the block where her car was parked.

"Here's my car." One of only a few left in the lot. The horn beeped as she aimed her clicker.

"See you at the hotel." Sebastian opened her door.

"Thanks."

"And, Miss Wentworth, please pray about what I said."

His words, almost a plea, echoed in her ears. *He needs someone like you in his life.* She'd once thought so, too.

"You're the one who quit, Desiree." Garrett tugged her arms from around his neck and backed away from her.

"I was angry. I'd obviously gotten emotionally attached to you and then I caught you with that groupie."

"Look, I appreciate everything you did for my career and I'm sorry for the way I treated you, but it was a long time ago. I was a kid." And she'd initiated their relationship, taking advantage of his broken heart.

"We could pick up where we left off. With business and pleasure." She stepped closer.

Garrett took another step back and signaled to security.

"I'm sorry, miss." A security guard cut her off. "I need to clear the room. Mr. Steele has an appointment."

"Really, Garrett? You're siccing security on me?"

"I'm sorry, Desiree. But I have an agent. I can give you a recommendation for your résumé."

"A recommendation." Her tone dripped sarcasm. "After all we were to each other? You'll regret this, Garrett Steele." She stalked away.

He blew out a big breath as Amanda marched toward him. From one woman's ire to another. He shot her his most charming smile, hoping to defuse her.

"Garrett Steele, you will not use Sebastian and me to secure your latest conquest." She propped her hands on both hips. "You didn't even ask us about dinner and I'm tired. All I want is to go to our room."

"I'm sorry, Amanda, but she wouldn't agree to have dinner with me alone. This one is different. She's not my latest conquest. Jenna is special." *She always has been.*

She pinned him with a knowing gaze. "I've known you a long time and you've thought every female you've ever laid eyes on was *special*."

"I know, but this one really is." Garrett chuckled. "You don't have to stay long, Mandy. Just until Jenna feels comfortable with me. I'll buy you something wonderful for the new house."

"I'll hold you to that, but you can't buy me." She smiled and linked her arm through his. "So tell me about her."

"We grew up together, from about the sixth grade all through high school."

"High school sweethearts?"

"Yes." Of the most serious kind. "She wanted to stay in Aubrey and I wanted to be a star. Our dreams didn't mix, so I had to choose." Had he made the right choice? After seeing her again, he wasn't so sure. In fact, he hadn't been so sure for a few years now.

"But you still have feelings for her." Her gaze narrowed, measuring him.

"How do you do that?"

"You've never taken anyone onstage before. And I saw the way you looked at her."

Had Jenna noticed how he looked at her? Why had he insisted she have dinner with him? To prolong the agony? He was leaving in the morning for the next stop on his tour. He couldn't even remember where that was.

"She still cares about you, too."

Garrett's steps stalled. "Why do you say that?"

"She didn't have to go onstage with you." Amanda shrugged.

A heart-deep grin tugged at his lips. One he couldn't wipe off if he tried. Jenna still cared.

Somehow, he had to hold on to her this time.

"So what about dinner?"

"Promise your intentions with this girl are completely honorable." She jabbed his shoulder with her finger.

He saluted her. "Boy Scout's honor."

How long had it been since he'd done anything honorable with a woman? But he wasn't that guy anymore. And he couldn't let Jenna Wentworth slip through his fingers again.

The valet opened her car door and Jenna handed him her keys. A chill wound around her. She pulled her suede jacket tighter and hurried into the spacious pillared lobby.

It was a little past midnight, and she wasn't hungry at all, but she'd driven to a fancy hotel to meet a man she barely knew anymore.

Yet he was so familiar. The man she'd connected with tonight seemed quite different than the image she saw of him on television. Like the old Garrett. The one who'd left her behind, because she'd expected him to give up his dream just as he'd expected her to abandon hers.

But something about him drew her to him. She couldn't rationalize it any more than she could rationalize why she had taken his hand at the concession stand tonight.

The hotel lobby was quiet this time of night. She'd been here a few times for design expos, appreciated the glamorous decor and knew her way around a bit.

But this was different. How to explain to the host whom she planned to meet? He'd surely think she was some groupie. She caught a glimpse of herself in a gilt-framed mirror. She looked the part.

Her top and black slim-fit jeans hugged her figure. As a designer, she loved interesting fabrics and textures, but, oh, to have worn something less flashy tonight.

She should have gone home and left Tori to find her own ride. So what if she'd promised to meet him?

Her stride faltered. She should leave now. Cut her losses.

But she'd driven Tori to Dallas; she couldn't leave her. Even though Tori deserved it.

And Garrett got to her. As usual. Despite all his fortune and fame, he was lonely. Did he regret leaving her behind?

Or would he get sidetracked with his groupie and forget all about her?

If he dared to stand her up after putting her through this, she'd throttle him. Or better yet, tell his mom.

She squared her shoulders and approached the woman at the desk.

"May I help you?"

"I, um… My name is Jenna Wentworth."

"Ah, yes, Trevor will escort you." The woman remained professionally aloof.

That went easier than expected.

"Right this way, ma'am." A man in a suit ushered her to the elevator.

No judgment in their eyes, but they probably thought Jenna was the flavor of the night.

Her stomach churned as the elevator began its ascent. Motion sickness—the last thing she needed. She needed all her faculties straight to face Garrett. Up. Up. Up. How far? Top floor? How many floors did the hotel have?

The elevator stopped. Finally.

The doors slid open and Trevor ushered her out. Thank goodness. She sucked in deep breaths as her stomach wobbled.

Trevor showed her to a meeting room where a server waited.

"Mr. Steele and the rest of his party are on their way. Would you like something to drink or an appetizer while you wait?"

"Iced tea, please. Sweet."

"Yes, ma'am."

The meeting room was huge. Large round tables occupied every available space and a wall of windows overlooked the city.

The soft lighting echoed that of the lobby with ivory walls and shimmering taupe damask tablecloths. Peach-and-taupe satin draped the chairs. The tables held glistening crystal glasses with gold-rimmed plates, and peach roses mingled with ivory carnations.

The waitress brought her tea, then left Jenna alone again.

How many women did Garrett bring to private meeting rooms each year? None. They probably went straight to his suite.

Her stomach turned. She shouldn't be here. Even if he'd changed, Garrett's lifestyle was nothing like hers and she couldn't imagine living the way he did. She grabbed her purse and darted for the door.

Just as it opened.

A man wearing a Dallas Cowboys cap stepped inside.

"I thought you might not show." Garrett took off his cap, removed his dark sunglasses and pulled his ponytail from his collar.

Her heart lodged in her throat. For the concert, he'd worn a black leather jacket and pants, but now he looked very at ease in his jeans and guitar-themed T-shirt. Like the guy she went to school with, but even better looking.

Clutching her purse. Had he caught Jenna on the verge of flight?

"Sebastian and Amanda will be along any minute." Garrett tugged his hair free of the coated elastic band. "Sorry it took me so long to arrive. Desiree held me up. She was my agent once and she's looking for a job." Among other things.

Jenna's gaze settled on his hair.

Probably should have left it hidden. He winced. His hair might be a bit much for Jenna's conservative sensibilities. Who was he kidding? His hair wasn't all that wasn't conservative—his wild years had been broadcast to the world.

Yet, she was still here. His heart skipped a beat.

But she'd changed, too. He couldn't imagine the Jenna he'd known wearing leopard skin. Even though it did crazy-good things to her golden eyes and tawny hair. Maybe she'd loosened up a little.

He wanted to touch her. To hold her and never let go. Not trusting his hands, he shoved them in his pockets. "So tell me about Jenna Wentworth."

"You've known me for years. There's nothing to tell." She cleared her throat and hugged herself.

Why was she so nervous? "Fill in the last eight years. How are your folks?"

"Still overprotective." She slowly walked the perimeter of the room, with ice clinking against the sides of her glass, and stopped to gaze out the endless windows overlooking the city. "It's an only-child thing. But Mama insists if she had thirteen kids, she'd worry as much about each one. If she knew the identity of my dinner companion tonight, she'd blow things all out of proportion."

He grinned. He could imagine Janet Wentworth in full protective mode. "And your dad?"

"Still the sweetest man in the world. So sweet, people take advantage of him. He never learned to say no."

Was she purposely keeping him at a distance? He strolled toward her, spanning the gulf, and stopped at her side. But he didn't even try to pretend the view interested him. "We might have the last two intact nuclear families in the world."

"It seems that way sometimes, doesn't it? I want that someday." Her cheeks pinked.

Me too. "Do you still live near them?"

"A horse pasture away. They tried to give the land to me, but I insisted on paying for it. Aubrey is peaceful." She shrugged. "No subdivisions for me."

She always rambled when she was nervous. Cute.

"I could never picture you in a subdivision. You'd plant some tree that dropped pods in your neighbor's yard and have the whole place in turmoil."

A hint of a smile curved her lips.

Garrett grinned. "It's a wonder you managed to move out at all. I remember your mama saying you couldn't move out before you turned forty-five, unless you got married, and you had to be thirty-five to do that."

She scurried to the next window. "So you have houses in Nashville and Orlando now and rarely get to come home due to your intense recording and touring schedules."

"You did your homework." Except for the more personal part. Several women had claimed to have given birth to his illegitimate child, but their claims had all been proved false. So far.

Though he'd left that scene, he wouldn't be surprised if his past caught up with him someday in the form of a child. His gut twisted.

Maybe Jenna didn't know all the gory details. He hoped not. But who was he kidding? She'd have to live on Venus not to have heard of his misdeeds.

One shoulder lifted. "I see your parents occasionally, and Tori is a huge fan, so she talks about you a lot. I'm surprised she left with your band. When she finds out we ate dinner together, she'll probably faint." She rolled her eyes. "Guess I better not tell her."

"So, I shouldn't consider you a fan?"

She cleared her throat. "I'd love to hear you sing a hymn again sometime."

A lump formed in his throat and he swallowed hard. "It's been a while since I've done that."

"Why?"

He sighed. "I never caught a break in the Christian industry, while the secular industry welcomed me with open arms."

"Do you ever go to church anymore?"

Pressure welled in his chest, the way it always did when he thought about God. "You sound like Amanda. She begs me to go to church with her and Sebastian every Sunday. No matter where we are and no matter what time I went to bed the night before."

"You should go."

Time to change the subject. "So why did you come to the concert?"

Her face went crimson. "Tori's license is suspended because she got a DWI and her cousin came down with the flu. She begged me to drive her, so I made her promise to go to church with me in return."

"You haven't changed a bit." He laughed. But a question burned in his chest. "Why did you take my hand in the lobby and go onstage with me?" He clutched the window frame.

"I'm not sure." The crimson shade deepened. "I guess I didn't want to embarrass you."

The air went out of his lungs. Maybe she didn't care. He pulled a chair at a nearby table. "Let's sit. I've been on my feet for hours."

She settled in the chair, her hands clasped in front of her.

"Since you know everything about me, tell me about your business." He claimed the seat across from her.

"I decorated a couple of doctors' offices and it took off. Most of my clients are in Denton, Fort Worth, Dallas, Garland and Rockwall. I've been looking into opening another store in the Galleria Dallas." She rolled her eyes. "Yes, Daddy set up a trust fund for me. But I want to expand on my own."

"Natalie said something about a second store at the car show last year. I'd hoped to see you when I was in Aubrey." There was a prolonged pause. Jenna seemed lost in thought.

"So tell me something I don't know about you." Her eyes flitted from his.

"I ran into the most interesting woman I've ever known today." He caught her gaze again. "She sits across the dinner table from me, as we speak, asking me to let her in on my secrets."

She cleared her throat. "I bet you tell all the women you meet how interesting you find them."

"I'm not playing you, Jenna." He turned her name into a caress. "I told you, I quit that scene a year ago."

The door opened and Amanda entered, followed by Sebastian.

"Ah, there you are." Garrett tried to sound happy to see them. "I was beginning to think y'all had stood us up." *Hoping, actually.*

"You know we'd never put you on the spot like that." Sebastian let his sarcasm shine through. "But I'm afraid we won't be joining you for dinner. We're too tired."

Reprieve. Jenna all to himself.

But Jenna's jaw dropped.

Would she bolt now that it was the two of them?

"Don't worry, honey." Amanda patted her shoulder. "You're safe with Garrett. He thinks the world of you."

The waitress arrived for their order.

Perfect timing.

Jenna ordered. But only a salad.

As the waitress left, Amanda covered a yawn. "I think the tour is wearing on me. I'll admit I'm glad it's almost over."

"I keep telling Amanda she wouldn't be so tired if she'd wear normal shoes," Sebastian teased.

"It's the only way I can reach my man." Amanda stretched up to plant a kiss on Sebastian's cheek.

Something twisted in Garrett's gut. To love someone like that. To be loved like that.

"It was nice to meet you, Jenna, and I hate to cut out on you. But I need to get this lady off her feet." Sebastian scooped Amanda up.

"What are you doing?" Amanda squirmed. "I can walk."

"Now you don't have to." Sebastian carried a giggling Amanda out.

"They're sweet together." Jenna's gaze narrowed. "But you, on the other hand, are not sweet."

Busted. Play innocent?

Garrett splayed both palms up. "What did I do?"

"You talked them into coming so I'd agree to join you?"

Might as well surrender. "Guilty as charged."

"I can't believe you dragged them out in the middle of the night."

"I didn't drag them out. Their room is right down the hall and I knew it was the only way you'd agree to have dinner."

The door opened and the server set their food on the table.

Jenna's eyes widened. "That was fast."

"Once Mr. Steele called to arrange the private dining room, we put his standard order in, and your salad didn't take any time, ma'am." She turned to Garrett, all business, not a hint of starstruck about her. "Can I get you anything else, Mr. Steele?"

"I think we're good."

"If you need anything, press the buzzer I gave you." She lit two candles on the table and turned away. The lights dimmed, leaving them in the flickering glow.

Jenna frowned.

"My eyes are always tired of bright light after a concert." Garrett cut a bite of his prime rib and shoved it into his mouth.

Jenna bowed her head. Her eyes closed.

Prayer. He hadn't even thought of it.

Several seconds passed before her head rose.

"Sorry." He sipped his tea. "I'm always starving after a performance since I don't eat before. Hard to sing on a full stomach."

Guilt pinged his gut. He used to pray over his meals.

But that was a lifetime ago. Back when God expected to hear from him.

He glanced at Jenna. Back when she'd been a part of his life, he'd never wondered who his real friends were or needed a bodyguard or realized fame wasn't worth losing Jenna Wentworth.

"I guess you don't like eating alone." She speared a tomato. "That's why this dinner was so important to you?"

"No." He covered her hand with his. "I couldn't let you pass through my life again without taking the opportunity to spend time with you."

Could she be the answer to an unuttered prayer?

A ripple bubbled in Jenna's stomach. Garrett wanted to spend time with her, but he no longer went to church or even prayed over a meal.

Her gaze dropped to the table. "How long have you known Sebastian and Amanda?"

"They were the first people I met in Nashville. I actually met them through my brother."

"How is Bradley? I usually see him every February when he does my taxes. Isn't Missy due soon?"

"Next month." Garrett nodded. "I planned my tour to finish in time for me to be there for my nephew's birth."

How sweet. Maybe he was still family oriented after all. Maybe the Garrett she knew still existed despite his career and reputation.

"He never mentioned doing work for you."

"Client privacy, I guess."

He captured her gaze again. She could drown in those eyes.

"What?"

"Nothing," she stammered. "I'd forgotten how green your eyes were. People in school always thought you wore colored contacts."

He leaned toward her—way too close. Her breath caught and her head swam as if she teetered on the edge of a cliff. She'd better watch her step.

Chapter 3

Mere inches separated her lips from Garrett's.

"What do you think?"

She cleared her throat. "I know they're real. You have your mother's eyes mixed with your dad's Cherokee coloring."

Focus on something other than his eyes. Her gaze shifted to his hair. So soft looking. Touchable. Oh, to bury her fingers in his hair and kiss him until she couldn't think straight. Who was she kidding? Simply looking at him turned her brain to mush.

"Does my hair bother you being so long?"

"Huh?" Her gaze met his again.

"I didn't grow it to be a rebel." He pushed it back from his face, pulling it into a ponytail before turning it loose to splay down his back. "After I'd been in Nashville awhile, I was so broke I couldn't even afford a haircut."

Her stomach tightened. Why did it hurt to think of him alone and hungry in Nashville? It had been his choice. To leave her behind. "Why didn't you tell your parents? They would have sent money."

"Too much pride. I didn't want to admit that my plan wasn't working. I'd moved to Nashville intent on starting a new Christian country genre and nobody was biting." Disappointment shone in his eyes.

So he did regret the turn his career had taken.

"Anyway, my hair kept growing, and I realized the longer it grew, the less it curled."

"I never understood why you hated your curls. Most women would kill for curls." She touched the hair near his cheek. Silky. She ran her fingers down the length of the strand. What was she doing? She jerked her hand away and clasped both hands in her lap as her face heated.

"So the length doesn't bother you?"

"No, but I'm surprised they didn't make you cut it when you got into country music. You don't fit the mold."

He frowned, then closed his eyes and leaned back in his chair.

She started breathing again.

"That's exactly what Desiree thought. She discovered me in some dive and got me a record deal. By then, I'd quit wearing my cowboy hat because it looked funny with long hair. Desiree thought my long hair and no hat would be a fresh concept for the industry."

"And it worked. Women across the country fell in love with the hot country star with the long hair."

A slow grin pulled up one corner of his mouth. "Hot?"

Was it warm in here or what? "I meant the next big thing— the newest rising star. You know." She stuffed a too-big fork-ful of salad into her stupid mouth.

As she concentrated on finishing her meal, one of his love songs began on the sound system. How much had he paid the server for her impeccable timing?

He stood and held out his hand. "May I have this dance?"

Oh, how she remembered dancing in his arms as he sang in her ear. They'd swayed to the soundtrack he'd recorded for their prom, chills running through her. He'd been asked to sing live, but he'd refused because he'd wanted to be her date. Proof that she'd once been his priority.

She trembled, longing to be in his arms. To dance with a backslidden Christian she was still in love with. What was she thinking?

Garrett's mere nearness played havoc on her comfort

zone. She couldn't take the chance of getting that close to him and keep her sanity. "I don't dance."

"Au contraire. I recall dancing with you at both of our proms."

"And I recall you always had straight A's in French class, while I never got the hang of it." His arms beckoned to her. Willing herself to stay seated, she concentrated on the song. But it was Garrett's song. "I also recall stepping on your feet at both of our proms."

"Dancing with you was worth sore toes."

As she forced her gaze away, the clock caught her attention. Almost two in the morning. "Please tell me that clock is wrong!"

"We missed the opportunity to kiss in the New Year last night." Garrett winked at her. "Want to make up for it?"

Her face singed. "It's been almost two hours. What about Tori?"

"Oh. I got sidetracked." He dug his phone out, jabbed a button and held it to his ear. "I need to talk to Rick." He grimaced. "I see. Thanks." He slid his phone back in his pocket. "Tori already left the party."

How dare Tori leave without her—after Jenna had spent almost two heart-shredding hours with Garrett so Tori would have a ride home. "Where did she go? Did she take a cab home?"

"No." His gaze stayed on the floor. "I'm afraid she left with Rick, one of the guys in my band."

A deep boiling started up in her chest.

"First she abandons me at the stadium and goes off to some party, and now she went with Rick to…" Her face scalded, as she stood and stalked back and forth across the room.

"Look, I'm really sorry. I should have made the call when I said I would. I completely forgot."

Because she'd sidetracked him.

"I can get you a room."

She shot him a glare.

"In a totally different hotel, if you want." Garrett held his palms toward her as if to ward off a blow. "You can pick up your wayward friend in the morning and go home."

"No." Her voice shook. "I intend to pick up my wayward friend tonight. I refuse to stay in a hotel room so she can... Tori and I will go home tonight and I may even fire her."

Garrett chuckled. "Simmer down now. I think it's illegal to fire an employee for after-hours behavior unless it interferes with their work. Is she scheduled to work tomorrow?"

"Lucky for her—no." She crossed her arms under her chest. "I should have fired her when she got the DWI." *But, no, I go and give her another chance and this is where it gets me.*

"Let me handle Tori." Garrett held up his hands again. "Hear me out. You don't know what you might find in Rick's room. Trevor will escort you to the private elevator and down to the parking garage. I'll have your car waiting, and one of my security team will bring Tori to you."

"I appreciate it." Her face would surely melt.

"The least I can do is spare you further embarrassment. I'm sorry. Some of my band members refuse to grow out of that stage."

"It's not your fault Tori has no morals." She huffed out a sigh. "Is Rick married?"

"I'm afraid so." His gaze dropped to the floor.

Had Tori even bothered to ask? Jenna closed her eyes. It probably made no difference to Tori. "I don't mean to speak badly of your friend, but I don't understand people. If they can't stay faithful to one person, why get married? Why not sleep around all they want? I mean, it's still not right, but it's better than cheating."

"I can't claim sainthood." Garrett shrugged. "But marriage is sacred."

Did she hear remorse? Did he regret his past? "So will I see you before I leave?"

"We booked the entire top floor, but I shouldn't take any chances at being seen with you in the hotel." His shoulders slumped. "Trust me, somehow it would find its way into the papers."

"Thanks for helping me with this…situation."

Garrett ponytailed his hair and tucked it into his collar, then slipped his sunglasses on and pulled his ball cap low. "Will I see you again?"

"Not unless you're in Aubrey." She managed a weak smile.

"Not this time. I visited with my family earlier in the week before the press got wind of me." He leaned close and his lips grazed her cheek. "May I call you?"

Tingling warmth engulfed her entire being.

Following her feelings could only lead to trouble. Example—Tori.

But now that she'd seen Garrett again, could she go back to life without him? Before she could stop herself, she nodded.

He cupped her cheek. His gaze locked on her lips.

Would he kiss her? Would she let him?

Jenna took a step back.

His hand fell to his side. "I'll look forward to talking to you, then. See you later, Jenna. This definitely isn't good-bye." He shot her one of his killer grins and stepped out the door.

Weak-kneed, she sank into the nearest chair. How had this happened? Garrett Steele back in her life. The guy who'd walked out on her. The guy who'd slept with countless groupies and supermodels and turned his back on God. What could they possibly have in common anymore?

Deep breath. In and out. She scooped up her purse.

The door opened and Trevor stepped inside. "Ready, ma'am?"

"Yes, thank you." She followed him out to the elevator. Her stomach roiled worse than before as they descended.

"Here we are, ma'am." The doors opened into the garage and a valet waited near her car a few steps away.

"Thank you."

"Anytime, ma'am."

No. There would never, ever be another time she would meet Garrett at a hotel. Ever.

Almost home. Jenna peered in her rearview mirror, but she couldn't see Tori sprawled in the backseat. "You okay?"

"Define okay," Tori moaned.

"I should have left you there."

"You'd never do that." Tori's words slurred together. "You're Jenna Wentworth. You never let anyone down and you always do the right thing."

"Sometimes I wish I didn't."

"No, you don't. Doing the right thing is what makes you— you." Tori's voice cracked and she started sobbing. "I love you, man."

"You're drunk." Jenna rolled her eyes. "And you won't remember any of this tomorrow."

"No, really, I love you, man."

"Can you walk?" Jenna pulled into her driveway and parked.

"Not sure?"

"Can you try?" Jenna got out and opened Tori's door.

Tori sat up and clutched her stomach. "I think I'm gonna be sick."

"Not in my car!"

Hanging her head out the door, Tori heaved.

Jenna jumped backward barely in time. Her stomach

twisted and she turned away until it was over. An hour ago, she could have killed Tori. But now she felt sorry for her.

"I'm done. Sorry." Tori staggered toward her. "Why are we at your house?"

"Because you're sick and you shouldn't be alone." Jenna put an arm around her. "But don't think this will get you out of church Sunday."

A distant, annoying ring. Jenna rolled over and pulled the satin pillow over her head. But it wouldn't stop. The phone.

She sat up and checked her caller ID. Natalie. Nine o'clock. On Saturday? Her only day to sleep in. Her cousin knew that. Why was she calling so early? She grabbed the handset to make it stop.

"Have you seen the news?"

"No. I was happily sleeping away my day off."

"Sorry, coz, but curious minds want to know."

"What?"

"Why on earth did you go to Garrett's concert?"

Jenna sat straight up. "How did you know?"

"It's all over the news."

"What?" Her heart plummeted.

"Imagine my shock when I see my cousin sitting on-stage with the guy she's loved since high school singing her a love song. Nice blouse, though."

"I don't love him. And you're teasing me. You were at the concert, so you saw me."

"Yes, you do love him. But, no, I wasn't at the concert."

"What channel?" She grabbed the remote off her night-stand and clicked the television on.

"That twenty-four-hour entertainment one you hate."

Jenna scanned through the channels. Her face filled the screen in a close-up. The camera panned back to show Garrett kneeling at her feet. Her stomach twisted in a tight ball.

"This can't be happening." She clicked the TV off, as if that would make it all go away, and covered her face with her hand.

"So what gives? Why did you go to the concert?"

"I have no idea."

"I'm coming over."

"Bring ice cream." She needed something to drown in. She hung up and the phone rang again. Caitlyn.

"Jenna, are you sitting down?"

"I know. I just got off the phone with your sister. What are you doing up so early?"

"Mitch woke me up when he saw the news."

"Natalie's bringing ice cream."

"I'm in."

Garrett rewound the clip. Again. Jenna. If he couldn't have her—at least he had the concert footage. He could watch it over and over, reliving the moment. Ridiculous.

How had he lived without her all these years? He hadn't. He'd tried. Tried everything to forget her. But he couldn't. And now that he'd seen her again, he had to win her back.

But she'd never be happy with touring. Where was he again? Oklahoma? Arkansas?

Oklahoma—yeah. Arkansas was next week.

A knock sounded at the door of his hotel room. "It's Andy."

"Come in."

Andy entered the room, his hands framing air like a camera lens. "This is big."

"Tell me you didn't leak to the press about the drunk girl and my dinner with Jenna. They'll turn the drunk girl on me and make my evening with Jenna something tawdry." He shot Andy a glare. "I won't have her smeared and I don't want that kind of rep anymore."

"This is bigger than that."

"What?"

"Your concert footage is all over the news."

"It always is after a concert."

"No, I mean the footage of you dragging that girl on-stage and singing to her."

His heart pounded. "What?"

Andy clicked the TV on.

His run with Jenna around the concert arena filled the screen. "We have to kill this."

"Are you crazy? Besides, we can't. It's gone viral."

"No—no—no." Garrett stood and paced the room. "This will ruin her life."

"How could this ruin her life? And it's not about the girl. It's about you. You've gone viral." Andy paced faster and faster. "Do you have any idea how your sales will spike? Women will buy concert tickets in hopes you'll drag them onstage with you. Women will buy CDs and fantasize it was them on that stage with you. You're a marketing genius."

"It had nothing to do with marketing, and if I'd thought about anything besides me—" Garrett flung a throw pillow at the big screen mounted on the wall "—I'd have never dragged Jenna into this. She's a private person. The media will pounce on her."

"More publicity for us."

"I have to call her." Garrett scrolled through his address book to her number.

"You have her number in your phone?"

"Completely off the record." Garrett jabbed a finger at Andy. "And if it gets leaked to the media, I'll be hiring a new publicist."

Andy shot him a hands-off gesture and left the room.

Busy signal.

Garrett sat down and ran both hands through his hair, pushing it out of his face. "What have I done? She'll never forgive me."

* * *

Both cousins flanked Jenna at her kitchen table. The off-white furnishings, creamy walls and cabinets with marble tiling usually soothed her. But today, not even the rich aroma coming from the coffeemaker or her favorite chocolate-chip ice cream melting in her mouth helped.

"What was I thinking?"

"What were you thinking?" Caitlyn scooped ice cream into her bowl. "I mean, when he was the entertainment at the car show here in Aubrey last year, you conveniently had to head for Dallas until he left. All these years, you've carefully avoided him and his concerts. But this time, you go. Why?"

"I told you. Tori—"

"Not buying it." Natalie pointed her spoon at Jenna. "You went because you wanted to see if the old feelings were still there. And they are. For both of you."

"Are not." Especially not for Garrett. "It was a stunt for publicity, nothing more." He'd as much as told her so afterward. She should have walked away then.

"It was obvious the way he sang that song to you. That lobby was full of willing women, but who did Garrett grab? You. A blast from his past."

"What are the odds?" Caitlyn splayed her hands. "Natalie reconnects with Lane, her high school sweetheart, last year. She was certain they couldn't overcome their past. But guess what? They did and they're married."

"Hopefully, there'll be a bun in the oven soon." Natalie patted her flat stomach. "And Caitlyn reconnected with her high school sweetheart last year. She never thought she could deal with Mitch's dangerous job, but guess what? She did, and they're getting married this summer."

"Haven't done any bun-planning yet." Caitlyn blushed. "First comes love, second comes marriage…"

"Then comes Jenna with a baby carriage." The cousins joined in singsong voices.

"Stop it." Her vision blurred. "Just because y'all ended up with your high school sweethearts several years after graduation, that doesn't mean I will. There's no hope for Garrett and me."

"Oh, sweetie." Natalie handed her a tissue. "We're sorry. No more teasing."

"And with God there's always hope." Caitlyn patted her arm.

"But that's the problem." Jenna wiped her eyes. "Garrett is so far away from God. And even if he was the old Garrett, the problem remains—I want to settle down and have kids. You can't do that on a concert tour."

"Well, it's not working out for you here in Aubrey, either." Natalie put her arm around Jenna. "God will work it all out, and if you're meant to be with Garrett—or someone new—you will be."

Not with Garrett. "In the meantime, what do I do about this concert footage? I had to take my phone off the hook because of all the calls from reporters. How did they get my number?"

"Hello?" Caitlyn shrugged. "You're, like, the last person I know our age who still has a home phone. You're in the book."

Jenna bit her lip. "Maybe now's a good time to have my home-phone service cut. I've got my cell and I'm at the store more than I'm home."

"This could be a gold mine of publicity for your store." Natalie arched one eyebrow. "This could be the pathway to your second store in the Galleria like you always wanted."

"Said like the great publicist you are." Jenna covered her face with both hands. "I want the second store, but not like this. I don't want publicity. I want my low-key, private life back."

"Then here." Natalie picked up the phone and plugged the cord back in, handing it to Jenna.

"Do they cut service on Saturday?"

"I want you to call Garrett."

"I can't call him. Why would I?"

"Because he'll know what to do to get the press off your back."

The phone rang in Jenna's hand. She jumped, then checked the digital screen. Mama.

She squeezed her eyes closed. "Hello."

"Jenna, I was flipping through channels and—"

"Tori had tickets and her cousin canceled at the last minute. She lost her license, so she begged me to drive her and promised to come to church with me in return."

A few seconds of silence ticked past. Would Mama buy her cover story?

"That doesn't explain what I saw on TV." Skepticism dripped from Mama's tone.

"I was in the lobby minding my own business. Garrett saw me and thought it would add to his concert."

"That's all?" Some of the doubt had ebbed.

Jenna crossed her fingers. "Uh-huh."

"I remember what a number he did on you, sweetie. And I don't want you to get hurt again."

"I'm fine. Natalie and Caitlyn are here."

"I'll let you get back to your company, then. See you at church tomorrow. And I'm proud of you for roping Tori into coming."

Jenna ended the call and blew out a big breath. The phone rang again.

A familiar number. Her eyes widened. "It's him."

"So answer it." Natalie splayed both hands upward.

"No."

"Then I will." Natalie grabbed the phone.

Jenna's stomach bottomed out and she dived for the phone. But it was too late.

"Hi, Garrett, Jenna's right here. She was just about to call you. Here she is." Natalie held the phone toward her.

Jenna shook her head.

"Talk to him," Natalie whispered.

Fingers trembling, Jenna pressed the phone to her ear. "Hello?"

Chapter 4

Garrett's heart turned to mush at the sound of her voice. He sank into the patio chair on his opulent hotel balcony. "You were about to call me?"

"We're all over the news."

"I know. I tried to call you. I'm sorry. My publicist leaked it."

"Well, I need you to unleak it."

His chest tightened. She hadn't been about to call because she wanted to talk to him. She only wanted damage control. "I wish I could. But it's gone viral."

"So what do we do now?"

"Wait for it to pass. Give it a week or so—there'll be another big story and your concert footage will be a thing of the past."

"'A week or so'?" Panic sounded in her voice. "I don't have a week or so. I've had my phone off most of the day because of reporters calling."

He'd been afraid of that.

"I can't run a business with my phone off or with so many reporters calling that my clients can't get through."

"There is one thing we can do." He stood and walked to the railing. The stone tiles were cool against his bare feet.

"What?"

"We could give them what they want."

"What do they want?"

"A story."

"I'm not some story."

"I mean, if we talk to them, explain there's no hot romance—" his voice cracked "—they'll go away."

"I'm not talking to the press."

"I'd be there with you. I've got a concert tonight in Oklahoma City and then a week later I have to be in Arkansas. I was planning to chill in between, but I can fit in a press conference." His doctor wanted him to rest his voice, but he'd cut his rest short for her.

"A press conference?" Her tone went an octave or two too high. "I want my quiet life back."

"A press conference would lay the story to rest. They'd see there's nothing going on between us—" his heart ached "—and move on to the next big story. It's either wait until the story blows over or a press conference and peace the next day."

Could he pull off a press conference with her? Could he convince the world he didn't love her? He had to—for her sake.

"No." She sighed. "Never mind. Sorry to bother you."

"You're never a bother. It was nice to hear your voice." He closed his eyes. "I'll call you again. I mean—just to talk?"

"If you can get through, go for it." A smile came through her words. Feminine laughter in the background.

"Sounds like I'll have to use your cell. Who answered the phone?"

"Natalie. She and Caitlyn are both here."

"Tell them I said hi."

"Sure."

"If you change your mind about the press conference, I'll be there. Just say the word." Anything to see her again. Spend time with her. Even if he had to tell the biggest lie he'd ever told. That he did not love Jenna Wentworth.

"Thanks anyway, but I need to go."

Her refusal stalled his heart. Obviously, she didn't want to see him again.

Jenna pushed End and the phone rang. A number she didn't recognize. Probably another reporter. She sighed and unplugged it again.

"Talking to the press would solve a lot of things." Natalie set her bowl in Jenna's sink and poured the three of them a cup of coffee without asking.

Maybe the steaming brew would wake her up from this bad dream.

"He suggested a press conference—with both of us."

"Brilliant." Natalie sipped her coffee.

"Not brilliant. How can talking to the press help?"

"*If* you can convince them there's nothing going on with Garrett, they'll move on. But that's a mighty big *if*. I'm not sure you could pull it off."

Jenna rolled her eyes. "There's nothing between us. I hadn't seen him in eight years until last night."

"I hadn't seen Lane in nine years, but all those butterflies took flight in my stomach with my first glimpse of him. Even after all our time apart."

"Same here." Caitlyn grinned. "Butterflies galore and I hadn't seen Mitch in ten years."

Jenna drained her coffee and stood up to get another cup. Movement outside her kitchen window skimmed her line of vision. A camera flashed. Jenna ducked and slid to the floor in front of the sink, facing her cousins.

"What are you doing?" Natalie frowned.

"There's a cameraman in my yard. He took a picture of me."

"This is crazy." Caitlyn hurried to the window.

"Get down." Jenna tugged on her jean leg.

"You can't be a prisoner in your own home." Caitlyn joined her on the floor.

"What now?" Natalie sat down on the other side of her.

"Maybe they'll get cold and go home." Jenna knew she was grasping at straws.

Vibration in Jenna's pocket. She dug her cell out. Garrett's number again.

"They're in my yard, Garrett." She whispered as if they could hear her.

"I was afraid of that. Don't worry—I've got you covered. I called to warn you I've got a couple of security guys on their way over."

"Thank you." Her stomach warmed.

"Not a problem. They'll stay until the press gives up."

"What if this siege lasts a week?"

"It probably won't, but I'm paying them."

"You shouldn't have to do that."

"I can afford it. And you're worth it. You're worth all the gold in the world to me."

His words curled around her heart.

"Garrett." A male voice in the background. "Come on. We gotta rehearse."

"I'd love to talk to you all day, but I gotta go. Rehearsal with the band."

Lyrics from "Beth" seared through her memory. The classic love song by the rock band Kiss had been a favorite. Until Garrett's long-ago words before he left for Nashville: *Will you be my Beth?*

A chill moved through her. No, she would never be Garrett's Beth. She would not endlessly wait for Garrett Steele to come home.

"Goodbye, Garrett."

"Goodbye? What happened to talk to you later?"

Music started up in the background.

"I don't think you should call me anymore."

"But you said I could." Hurt rang in his tone. "Just to talk."

"Come on, Garrett," a male voice called.

"You need to go."

"Not until we get this settled. You said I could call you."

"That was before the press camped out in my yard. It's better if we cut all ties."

"But—"

"Garrett!" The male voice in the background again. More insistent this time.

"I'm coming," he snapped.

"Goodbye, Garrett." She pressed End and closed her eyes.

"You okay?" Caitlyn's elbow nudged her in the ribs.

"Fine."

"You're crazy." Natalie sighed.

"I was crazy to get anywhere near him again. He's sending a couple of security guys over to keep the reporters at bay."

"And you honestly think it's better this way?" Caitlyn settled a hand on her arm.

"Yes." Who was she kidding? Seeing him again had stirred up all the feelings she'd long tried to bury. There was no getting over Garrett Steele. Ever.

"Um." Tori stood in the doorway with her hand pressed to her forehead. "Is this some kind of weird family pow-wow?"

Jenna had almost forgotten her guest.

"Get down." Jenna jabbed her finger at the floor.

Tori slid to the floor right where she was. "What's going on?"

A fit of laughter bubbled up inside Jenna. They must look ridiculous lined up against the sink cabinet. Yet, it wasn't funny.

"Morning, Tori." Caitlyn smiled as if nothing were amiss.

"It was late when we got home last night, so Tori stayed here."

"Sorry about…everything." Tori's gaze dropped to the floor.

"Come on, Nat. Let's go in the living room." Caitlyn— on all fours—crawled in that direction.

Natalie giggled but followed. "This reminds me of Grandma Wentworth crawling all over her house every night because some doctor told her it was good exercise."

After the crawling convoy disappeared down the hall, Jenna got on her knees, poured Tori a cup of coffee and scooted over beside her.

"So, how do you feel?"

"Like somebody pumped paint stripper into my head." Tori's hand shook as she took the coffee cup. "Thanks for letting me stay."

"No problem."

"Anybody else would have left me in Dallas and let me find my own way home."

"Probably."

"So, why didn't you?"

"Because I care."

Tori swiped a tear away. "I'm dying to know why we can't stand up."

Gravel crunched outside.

"More family coming to crawl around with us?" Tori sipped her coffee.

"No."

A car door slammed, followed by chatter from several voices. Several motors started, and more gravel crunched. The rumble of engines faded in the distance and finally, blessed silence.

"I think it's over now." Jenna stood and peered out the window. Nothing. She took Tori's cup and helped her stand. "I'm under attack. By reporters."

"Because of the concert?"

"If you dare to even think this is cool or talk to any re-porters, I'll kill you."

"Please do." Tori closed her eyes. "Put me out of my misery."

"Why don't you go back to bed?" Jenna put her arm around Tori's shoulders.

"Best idea I've heard in ages." Tori hung on to Jenna as if she were a lifeline.

Jenna wasn't. But she knew just the lifeline Tori needed. And it would be easy if Tori stayed another night.

At the back of the sanctuary, Jenna took a deep breath. Nothing like church to calm the nerves and forget your worries. Why couldn't everyone realize Jesus was better than any drug or drink?

Wearing one of Jenna's dresses, Tori, usually self-assured and confident, clutched the back pew. White-knuckled, as if she might bolt any second rather than go any farther.

At least they hadn't had to fight reporters to get here. Thanks to two beefy security guys camped in Jenna's yard this morning.

"Come on." She linked her arm through Tori's and pro-pelled her friend forward. *Please, Jesus, do Your work on her.*

"Can't we sit in the back?"

"I usually sit on the fifth pew. It won't kill you."

Several people welcomed them and she introduced Tori. No one mentioned the concert ordeal. A teenage girl darted in her direction, but the girl's mother called her back.

Close call. She didn't want to talk about Garrett. Or think about him. Or even acknowledge his existence.

For the first time in—she couldn't even remember when—she'd missed Sunday school. But there'd been no way she could have gotten Tori going any earlier.

Her parents, uncle and aunt, and Caitlyn and Mitch, lined her family pew—everyone except Lane and Natalie, who attended a different church.

"Jenna." Mama's eyes held worried questions. Questions Jenna didn't want to answer. "Are you okay?"

"I'm fine." She managed a big smile. "You remember Tori?"

"I'm still reeling from finding out Jenna knew Garrett Steele." Tori giggled.

And reeling from something else. Jenna wasn't sure if it was drugs or alcohol. *Must have a stash in her purse.* Jenna's blood burned. What if they'd gotten in a fender bender this morning?

She filed in and sat by Caitlyn, leaving room for Tori next to her mom.

"Aunt Millie's here again," Caitlyn whispered. "She's still not a Christian. Pray she'll hear something that'll change her mind."

Caitlyn and Natalie's aunt had gotten involved in an abusive relationship, been missing for thirty years and only recently come home to reunite with her grown son. "I'll help you pray for Millie and you help me pray for Tori."

"Done. We're all going to lunch afterward. Natalie and Lane are coming once their service ends. Maybe you and Tori can join us."

"Sure." After she made Tori empty her purse. She'd warn her cousins—not one word about Garrett. Jenna blew out a big breath. *Concentrate on Jesus. And Tori.*

The piano player began a hymn and everyone took their seats. She sent up a prayer for Tori and Millie as the song service began. Three hymns later, the music faded away and the pastor approached the pulpit.

Jenna watched Tori from under her lashes throughout the entire service. As the pastor poured out the message of salvation through Christ, Tori seemed bored—picking at her nails, her gaze downcast. Was she even listening?

The altar call came and her cousins' aunt went forward and knelt. At least one soul had been stirred. Tori seemed unfazed by it all.

The baby grand in the corner of his suite tugged at Garrett. He settled on the bench and picked out a melody. His fingers followed the notes without him even thinking. *"Amazing Grace."* His hands stilled. Why was he thinking about such things? That was a long time ago.

But since he'd seen Jenna again, he'd been thinking a lot about the past, what used to matter and how simple his life had once been.

The hot tea with honey failed to soothe his raw throat. Somebody must have shoved a bottle cleaner down his throat while he slept. Maybe he should have taken his doctor's advice and ended the tour early to rest his voice. He longed for a glass of iced, sweet tea, but Amanda swore by this elixir.

Back-to-back concerts for the past two nights had done him no favors. But at least he didn't have another concert for five whole days. Oklahoma for five days. He didn't know a soul in Oklahoma, and even if he did, he was a prisoner in his hotel room no matter what state the hotel happened to be in.

His phone buzzed, doing a vibrating dance across the bench beside him. He grabbed it before it fell. Jenna's number.

"Jenna?" His surprise echoed in his tone.

"I had reporters everywhere." Panic laced her voice. "The police had to come."

"What about my security guys?"

"At my store, Garrett. At the Stockyards. My store was crawling with reporters. My customers couldn't get in."

He ran a hand through his hair. "I'll send more security guys to cover your store."

"And then they'll find out where I go to church. And where I grocery shop."

"Sounds like one exciting life you live." He tried to lighten things up with a chuckle.

"I can't live like this, Garrett." Her voice broke on the verge of tears.

"I'll hire a bodyguard."

"That's ridiculous."

"I want to help you." He stood and paced the large suite. "I got you into this mess."

"I give. I'll do the press conference."

Garrett couldn't contain his smile. Even though she was upset and he'd caused her problems, this meant he'd see her again. Soon.

"I'll set everything up and get back with you."

"Soon, Garrett. Make it soon."

"ASAP. You're at the top of my priority list." Where she should have been all along.

"In the meantime, I guess I'll take you up on more security."

"Done."

"Thanks." The line went dead.

Now all he had to do was find a neutral zone for the press conference. And contact the media. He needed someone in the know.

Natalie.

They'd talked at the Aubrey Car Show last spring and she'd given him her card. He scanned the address book in his phone. Had he kept her number?

Yes. He punched the number in.

"Natalie Gray, publicist. How may I help you?"

"I need someone in the know to set up a press conference for me."

"I'm assuming this is Garrett."

"Sorry, I forget the pleasantries when I'm on a mission."

"Don't you have a publicist?"

"He's the one who leaked the concert footage of Jenna to the press. He doesn't know it yet, but he's fired as soon as I reach him. Know any good publicists?"

She laughed. "I'm already employed by the Fort Worth Stockyards."

"I'll pay more."

"Does the name Wentworth ring a bell? Money doesn't talk to me."

"Jenna's agreed to a press conference. I've ruined her life and I need you to help me with damage control."

Several seconds of silence ticked past. *Must have gotten her attention.*

"We'll talk. In the meantime, give me a date and time. I'll set things up and get back with you."

"Thanks, Nat."

Now all he had to do was convince the world he didn't love Jenna. Tall order.

Four miserable days since making the stupidest decision of her life had landed Jenna here with her privacy up for public consumption. The world's biggest honky-tonk, Billy Bob's Texas, for a press conference.

With Garrett.

Jenna hadn't been here since local bull rider Clay Warren retired. She'd gone to school with Clay, and following his career had been fun. And now they were family, sort of, since her cousin had married his.

Kendra, photographer extraordinaire and Natalie's best friend, dusted powder across Jenna's nose with a big fluffy brush.

A tickle started and her eyes watered. "Ah ah ah achoo."

"Oh, dear." Caitlyn dabbed under Jenna's eyes with a sponge. "There. All fixed."

Jenna looked in the lit bathroom mirror. Garish makeup—way overdone. She barely recognized herself and grabbed a tissue. "It's way too much."

"All the lighting makes everybody look pale." Natalie swiped the tissue away from her. "Trust Kendra—she knows what she's doing. It's perfect for the camera. All you need is to undo a couple of buttons."

"No." Jenna clasped a hand to her brown silk blouse, buttoned all the way to the throat. "I'm going for conservative." She'd chosen the plain taupe suit on purpose. If she looked nothing like Garrett's type, maybe she could pull this off.

"But there's conservative and there's downright uptight." Natalie fluffed Jenna's hair. "All this brown will look blah on the screen."

"I'm fine." Jenna spun the chair and stood.

"I'm not finished." Natalie aimed her hairspray can like a weapon.

"I am. You'll make me sneeze again." Jenna blocked Natalie's aim with both hands. "I appreciate your help, but I'm not used to all this primping. I'm sorry. I know y'all are only trying to help. But I'm done."

"Calm down." Caitlyn laid a hand on Jenna's arm. "The camera will love you."

Jenna huffed out a sigh and exited the bathroom with no clue where to go. But Garrett leaned against the wall, looking like one of those cowboy silhouettes people put in their yards. Only three-dimensional and downright dangerous in his olive *Don't mess with Texas* T-shirt, worn jeans and his customary rattlesnake boots.

"Ready to get this show on the road?" He took her hand in his.

She trembled.

"Don't be nervous." He squeezed her fingers. "You'll do great. America already loves you."

If only he loved her, too.

Where did that come from? If she let those thoughts run wild, how would she convince America they were only friends?

Why oh why oh why had she gone to that concert? Yes, Tori had come to church with her, but it hadn't seemed to do any good. And Jenna's life had come unwound.

"I can't do this." She stopped. "I'm a nervous wreck and we haven't even started yet."

"Settle down." Garrett ran his hands up and down both her arms. "Yes, you can. You want your life back, right? Just follow my lead."

Her nerves went into overdrive at his touch.

"I'll do all the talking. Natalie and my security guys will get you out of here before the questions start."

"So they won't ask me anything?"

"Some reporters are pros at twisting words, so I thought I'd spare you."

She made the mistake of meeting his gaze. Drowning in a sea of green—her brain flatlined.

"Sorry to interrupt, lovebirds." Natalie clapped her hands. "But if y'all go on camera looking at each other like that, we'll never pull this thing off."

"Right." Garrett let go of her and didn't reclaim her hand.

"Why are we doing this at Billy Bob's?"

"Garrett has news other than your supposed nonromance." Natalie grinned. "You'll see."

Garrett ushered her out into the Texas Club meeting room. An extended bar with etched glass behind it and stuffed wild-game heads mounted on the walls gave the room a saloon feel. A portable stage had been erected at one end of what was usually a dance floor.

Reporters with microphones inscribed with all the local news stations' call letters jostled for position as Garrett ushered her up the steps toward a podium. Her mouth went dry. She. Could. Not. Do. This. Jenna turned to bolt.

Chapter 5

Panic flashed in Jenna's eyes and Garrett blocked the exit in case she got any ideas of escape. He shot her a reassuring smile and hung back to let Natalie begin the conference.

"Ladies and gentlemen, thank you for coming. I'm Natalie Gray, Garrett Steele's new publicist."

"When did that happen?" Jenna's gaze swung from Natalie to Garrett.

"I'll tell you all about it later," he whispered.

"Mr. Steele is here to make an important announcement and then he'll take a few questions."

Garrett stepped up to the microphone. But Jenna stood as if rooted to the floor. He turned toward her and almost took her hand. No. He couldn't do that if he was going to convince the world he didn't love her. He waved her forward instead.

Though she stepped up beside him, he knew she wanted this over. For her life to return to normal. For him to fade into her past. Not brighten up her future.

"Thanks for coming, everyone." He cleared his raw throat. "First, I wanted to clear something up. Y'all know Jenna Wentworth. Thanks to my antics, she's now a household name and the media has conjured up a nonexistent romance between us." His stomach twisted. How could he stand here and turn the way he felt about her into nothing? But he had to. For her sake.

"So Jenna and I are here to set the record straight." He

paused. Five, six, seven seconds turned it into a dramatic pause. "Jenna and I are high school friends. That's all."

Garrett's throat closed up. He turned to face her and his gaze held hers a few seconds. More than anything, he wanted to tell her exactly how he felt. But he couldn't. It wouldn't do any good anyway. She was obviously over him. He focused on the reporters.

"We've known each other since middle school, but Jenna's life is in the Fort Worth area and mine is—" he laughed, hoping to break his own tension "—all over the place. Sometimes, I can't even remember what city I'm in when I wake up in the morning." And it was getting old. He looked forward to his upcoming break.

If only he could spend his break with Jenna.

"Jenna and I hadn't even seen each other in eight years until she came to my concert as a friend, to support my career. I'm the one who saw her and dragged her onstage for fun." Garrett pushed his hair away from his face. *Should have ponytailed it.* "But if you need a great interior decorator, Jenna has a store right here at the Stockyards—over on East Exchange—across from Cowtown Coliseum."

Laughter rippled through the sea of reporters.

"Now Jenna's going to leave because she has a business to run." He gave her a quick hug. Like a friend would do. Oh, how his arms wanted to retrieve her as she waved to the crowd and turned away.

"Now, on to my announcement." Garrett scanned the crowd. "As y'all know, I'm wrapping up this tour. My final concert was supposed to be next weekend in Atlanta, but I've decided to add one more stop. On January eighteenth, I'll be right here at Billy Bob's for a special concert."

Applause and wolf whistles erupted. Hopefully, they'd forgotten all about Jenna. He wanted to turn and search for her, but he needed to let her fade into the background.

Natalie stepped up beside him. "You heard it first here at Billy Bob's, folks. Garrett has time for a few questions."

"Hi, Garrett." A female reporter raised her hand.

She looked familiar.

"I have it on good authority since I went to high school with you and Jenna that you were in love with her back in high school. Everybody thought y'all would end up married."

Gasps and mumbles moved through the crowd.

Maybe this hadn't been such a good idea. Sammie Sanderson, he remembered now. She'd headed up all the gossip in their high school days. And now she'd gone pro.

"Yes." Garrett swallowed hard. "Jenna and I had a high school romance. Emphasis on *high school.* We were young."

"But neither of you have ever married. You sure there isn't still a spark there?"

"No spark. Jenna and I went our separate ways long ago."

"Well, if you're *friends*—" Sammie's tone was loaded with sarcasm "—will you keep in touch?"

"Let me rephrase." *Please somebody other than Sammie come up with a question about anything other than Jenna.* "We were high school friends. We lead very different lives now. We're both focused on our careers, which leaves little time for long-distance friendship. Or anything else."

"But your tour is almost over." Sammie smirked. "Will you spend your break in Aubrey? Near Jenna? And your family, of course."

"If I told you where I'm spending a break, it wouldn't be a break, now would it? My family and I are planning to travel."

Finally, another female reporter raised her hand. "Why did you decide to tack the Billy Bob's concert onto the end of your tour?"

Was she suspicious? Catching on that the announcement was geared toward getting the spotlight back on him instead of Jenna? Could this woman know his Billy Bob's concert had only been set up last night?

"Because it's home. Billy Bob's was one of the first places I appeared in concert. It seemed like a great place to end this tour. But I didn't think of it until I spent a few days with my family in the area before my Dallas concert. And then it took some time for my publicist to get things set."

"Why the new publicist?" a man shouted.

"Let's just say you can't believe everything you've heard about me over the years. I'm much tamer these days and I wanted someone with a fresh perspective on my career and personal life. I've also known Natalie since middle school and I ran into her at the car show in Aubrey last year. The wheels started spinning then."

His throat felt as if it were on fire and he gulped from his water bottle.

"When does the next tour kick off?" a man yelled.

If there *was* another tour with the way his throat felt. "Final details aren't in place yet." He bumped Natalie's elbow, his signal to wrap things up.

"I'm afraid that's all the time we have." Natalie took control. "Mr. Steele appreciates everyone coming. Tickets are on sale now for the Billy Bob's concert."

Garrett turned away, thankful for the four security guys waiting. Had they bought his story? Would they leave Jenna alone now? Could *he* leave her alone?

Clutching a lacy pillow to her stomach, Jenna clicked the TV off. Utterly humiliated. Every local station had aired sound bites from the press conference. Garrett had belittled their *high school* romance for the whole world. As if their feelings for each other had been nothing.

It hadn't meant nothing to her.

Wasn't this what she wanted? Garrett would leave and

her life would get back to normal. She was better off without him.

So, why did she feel so lonely?

The phone lay on the coffee table. Her fingers itched to pick it up and call him. She could thank him for the press conference.

No. She needed to cut all ties. She had to.

The phone wasn't even on. Would the reporters stop calling now? She picked up the handset and flicked the ringer button on.

Nothing. Maybe her siege was over. Only ten missed calls since she'd cleared it this morning before heading to the press conference. She set the phone back on the table gently, as if setting it down too hard would make it start ringing again.

Now, if she could get back to normal. Forget her brief interlude with Garrett. His touch. His eyes. His lips.

She buried her face in her hands.

The phone pealed and she jumped, then checked the caller ID.

Garrett.

Her hands shook. *Don't answer.* She pressed her hands underneath her thighs lest they betray her.

Four rings. She grabbed it. "Hello?"

"Jenna, I wanted to make sure you were okay. Are you at your store?"

"No, I was a nervous wreck, so I came home." She pressed a hand to her heart, willing it to slow. Why did the mere sound of his voice set her aflutter? "Tomorrow everything should be settled down. I'll go in then."

"I'm really sorry about all this."

"I know. I think it'll be okay now."

"Have you seen the footage?"

"Yes."

"Jenna." His voice did wonders with her name. "I told

them what I had to—to get them to leave you alone. Remember what I said—you can't believe everything you hear in the media. I couldn't tell them the truth. Back then, you were everything to me."

Her breath caught. What about now? "I appreciate your help with this. You said you'd tell me how Natalie got involved?"

"My former publicist had a skewed view of things." Garrett sighed. "Any publicity was supposed to be good publicity. He leaked things to the press over the years. Some of it wasn't even true. I put up with it too long. Giving the press your concert footage was the final straw."

Protecting her. Something in her stomach warmed.

"Natalie loved the Stockyards job." She curled her legs up beside her on the couch. "You must have made her an offer she couldn't refuse."

"Actually, we compromised. She's still the Stockyards publicist. I'm just another client." He cleared his throat. "Speaking of the Stockyards, I'm attending the Hall of Fame induction the night before my Billy Bob's concert. Are you planning to come?"

No. No. No. Must he invade every corner of her life? "Actually, I am. As a guest of Clay Warren since Caitlyn married his cousin."

"Mitch and I keep in touch, but that one shocked me. Proof that high school romances can reignite."

Stop toying with my heart.

"Then I guess I'll see you at the ceremony. I can still call you, right?"

She couldn't take it. Not one more flirtatious statement. Not one more flash of those intense eyes. Not one more touch she couldn't forget. "Look, Garrett, it's been nice seeing you again, but I think it would be better if we go our separate ways."

"Why?"

"We did the press conference to snuff publicity about us. I don't want to get it started up again, and I'd appreciate it if you don't speak to me at the induction ceremony since the press will be there." Could she pull off ignoring him if they ran into each other?

"No one will know if we talk on the phone."

I will. And her heart had already begun to hope. No. She was an adult. With a brain. She could be Garrett's friend. This was an opportunity to remind him he still needed God.

"Jenna, you still there?"

"You can call me. But we're friends. That's all."

"Then I'll talk to you later, friend."

Their connection ended, but a full five minutes passed before her pulse returned to normal.

Garrett reclined his chair as his private jet cut through the clouds. What state? Where were they headed? He wasn't sure anymore. He rewound the concert footage again and pushed Play. Again.

The only thing he had left of Jenna. Other than hearing her voice on the phone. He couldn't live like this. Since he'd seen her again, touched her again, she was like a drug. He wanted more.

Only a week since he'd seen her, but the longest week of his life.

His phone rang and he dug it out of his pocket. Natalie. He paused the concert footage on a tight shot of Jenna's face.

"Is Jenna okay?"

"She's fine. Now, why is that the first thing you ask when I call?"

"Just wondering if the reporters were still bothering her."

"Yeah, right." Natalie laughed. "They scattered sniffing for their next story. Jenna's back at her store designing her little heart out. And business is booming."

"Good."

"I got an interesting phone call, though. Do you know a Desiree Devine?"

Her name twisted his insides into a knot of regret. "She called you?"

"Please tell me she's not some hooker from your past. Her name certainly sounds like one."

"Believe it or not, that's her real name. She discovered me. My first agent." His first in a lot of areas. She'd offered her bed, comfort and alcohol when he was still grieving Jenna. And set him on a destructive path. But he couldn't blame his bad choices and sins on her.

"She wanted your number, so I told her I'd give you her number."

"I don't need it."

"Okay. On to item number two. Why don't you have a video for 'One Day'?"

"It wasn't the projected hit for this album. But people started using it for weddings and it caught on."

"It's past time for a video. I was thinking we could do a reenactment of the concert run with you dragging Jenna onstage."

"Brilliant." His heart went double time. "Do you think we have any chance of convincing her to do the video?"

"Hold on. I wasn't thinking of Jenna. I was thinking an actress—she can look like Jenna."

"Why not Jenna?"

"Because we just got her out of the spotlight."

"Let me at least ask her."

A sigh drifted through the line. "What are your intentions with my cousin?"

"I love her. I've never stopped."

"So what was with all the women?"

Garrett winced. "I'd love to say none of it was true. Not all of it was, but enough. I guess I was trying to forget her."

"You can't hurt her, Garrett. Not again."

"I have no intention of hurting her."

"So say you talk her into the video." Natalie's tone took on a stern warning. "What happens after that? You start another tour and leave her behind. Again."

"Does she still love me?"

"No way am I going to answer that. Answer my question."

He sipped his hot tea with honey. "What if there isn't another tour?"

"Is your throat that bad? Maybe we shouldn't do a video."

"I'm sure I'll be fine by then." He put all the confidence he could into his tone.

"I want you to see your doctor as soon as the tour is over. He'll run tests and we'll see what the problem is. It could be strain."

Garrett squeezed his eyes closed. "I hope so."

"I'm praying so."

That touched him, more than he could say. "Promise me you won't tell Jenna I still love her."

"I already told Jenna you still love her, but I won't tell her you said it. You need to tell her."

Fireworks went off in his chest. "You told her? What did she say?"

"She didn't believe me. Back to my question. What if your throat turns out fine? Will you keep touring?"

"Probably. But maybe not as long. Maybe Jenna and I could be together if I were home more."

"I'll tell you one thing—you can't have groupies and Jenna."

"I haven't been with anyone in a year. Honest."

"Wow."

"It got old."

"I actually know the feeling." Silence for a few seconds.

"Well, you're gonna have to get it straight with God before Jenna will even think about seeing you again."

Could he do that? If he'd never accepted Christ, it would be different. But he'd known the truth and turned his back on God. Could God get past his past?

"Let me know what she says about the video. But I wouldn't hold my breath. We'll wait on scheduling until you see your doctor, and in the meantime, I'll start looking for actresses."

"Will you help me talk her into it?"

"I can try. But she doesn't listen to me. Especially where you're concerned."

Why should she? He'd abandoned her.

Just like he'd abandoned God.

In her element, Jenna hummed as she led a client down the aisle of shelves stocked with ready-made comforters bearing her name, the *Wentworth Collection.*

Two weeks since the press conference and life was back to glorious normal. Except, dagnabbit, she missed him.

"I didn't realize you had your own line." The woman sounded impressed.

"Everything you see in the store is my own design." She gestured to the lamps, sculptures and wall art.

"It's all very nice. But I was hoping for something less… cowboy inspired."

"Actually, I'm the same way. I have a more elegant line over here."

The lady ran her hand over a luxurious cream-and-gold brocade comforter. "I like this much better. But I think I'd like something unique. The sign outside said something about exclusive designs."

Stay calm. Jenna's breath caught. *Don't let her know she's making my day.* "Yes, I have a custom-made service. You can pick your fabric swatch. We do curtains, comforters and design accents to go with whatever you choose. We also recover furnishings."

"That's what I want."

This was where she usually lost them. Jenna handed her a catalog with pricing. "Of course, custom is more expensive and it depends on the fabric you choose."

The woman flipped a few pages. "Very reasonable for custom. How long will it take?"

Jenna did a mental happy dance. "It depends on what you order, but two weeks at the most."

"I'd like to see the swatches."

"Of course." Jenna's smile went heart deep as she led the woman to the back of the store.

Over the next half hour, they picked fabric and lining for a comforter, curtains and recovered love seat. After selecting accessories, the woman paid the deposit. "I'm sorry I kept you after closing."

"No problem. I'm glad you found what you were looking for." Jenna unlocked the door and let her out, then slid the dead bolt back into place.

"Yes." She let herself do the happy dance for real this time.

The clock gonged six times, then clanged softer for the half hour. She closed the blinds and hurried to tally the register.

With the drawer balanced and a deposit ready, she started turning off lights.

A knock sounded at the front door. Jenna frowned. Caitlyn? Or maybe the custom-order lady needed something else.

She hurried to the door and peeked through the blinds. A cowboy peered back at her. She jumped.

Even though it was dark outside, he wore sunglasses. A chill crawled over her skin.

"I'm sorry. We're closed."

"I know."

Garrett? No sign of his hair under the cowboy hat. And Garrett didn't wear cowboy hats anymore. Her ears were only wishing. Despite her brain.

The man lowered his sunglasses a bit. Enough for her to get a glimpse of those gorgeous green eyes.

Chapter 6

"What are you doing here?" Her voice sounded high.

"Let me in before someone recognizes me."

She unlocked the door and he hurried inside, then she slid the bolt back in place.

"Do you always work after dark?"

"I got caught up with a client. I usually close at six o'clock during the week and eight o'clock on the weekends."

"You should close the blinds before dark." He removed his sunglasses and uncustomary cowboy hat. His hair fell free and her heart took a tumble with it. "Anybody can see inside. See that you're alone. I watched your little celebratory dance and everything."

Her throat constricted. "You were watching me?"

"I had to make sure no one else was here." He shrugged. "So what were you celebrating? Good day?"

"A great day. I'm drowning in a sea of ready-made cowboy couture, but I've been getting a lot of custom orders with nothing cowboy in sight."

"I must admit I was surprised to learn you had a store here. The Stockyards doesn't fit your style."

"The Galleria Dallas is my dream." She smoothed her hand over a crushed-velvet fabric. "But it's so expensive. Caitlyn has a clothing store three spaces down and told me this spot was available. Natalie thought it would be a good place to launch Worthwhile Designs."

"But if you don't like cowboy, why design it?"

For a lot of the same reasons you ended up singing country love songs instead of country gospel. "I tried my elegant line and custom designs. I had a few sales, but not enough to keep up with the overhead."

She shrugged. "Natalie, the marketing whiz, pointed out the problem—my store didn't fit the Stockyards brand because people come here looking for cowboy. My Western line pays the bills." Why was she standing here answering his twenty questions while he hadn't answered hers? "Why are you here?"

"I flew in a day early for the Hall of Fame ceremony. I thought I'd come see your store. Have you show me around and tell me all about it."

Her heart tugged in his direction. "I started my own ready-made line. I have cowboy and elegant, but in the past, the cowboy has outsold by far."

"You have your own line?"

"Of bedding and bath, curtains, accessories, throw pillows, kitchen linens. Everything you see in the store is my design."

"Very impressive." He ran his hand along the side of his face.

His scruffy beard made her want to do the same. Or better yet, rub her cheek against it.

"You know, I might have an idea on how you could launch a store at the Galleria."

"I'm not using my trust fund. I haven't so far and I won't start now."

"That's not what I had in mind. Natalie called me today with a great idea."

Great. Her cousin was conspiring with Garrett against her. "I knew her being your publicist would come back to haunt me."

Garrett grinned and her heart took flight. Right out of her chest.

"She thinks I should re-create our concert run with an actress in a video for 'One Day.'"

Her heart thudded on the floor. Why should it bother her for him to act out *their memory* with some beautiful woman?

"But I think it would be better with the original star."

Me? Her gaze collided with his. She shook her head. "Absolutely not."

"Why?"

"We had to do a press conference to get the media off my trail. I don't want to stir that up again."

"But think of all the publicity. How has business been since the concert?"

"Crazy. I've got more custom orders right now than ever before. I may have to hire more help."

"Do you think that would have happened without the concert?"

She turned her back on him. "I don't know."

"I'm not saying you couldn't be successful on your own. You're extremely talented, Jenna. But publicity definitely has its perks."

"I won't lose my life again." She hugged herself. "Everything just settled down."

"We put the romance rumors to rest and this doesn't have to stir them up." He turned her to face him, his hands resting on each of her upper arms. "Natalie can set up an interview for me. I'll let the video concept out of the box and explain how our concert run caused such a buzz, it seemed the perfect setup. And how we originally planned to use an actress, but since we're friends, I asked you to play yourself."

She focused on the third button down from his throat. "I've never done anything like that. I can't act."

"Think about it. Think about oceans of satin and velvet in an upscale store with marble pillars in the Galleria."

"No fair using my dream against me."

"Let me make your dreams come true, Jenna."

Her gaze met his, but his dropped to her lips.

The opening notes of "One Day" played.

A welcome interruption. But did it have to be *that song?* Jenna stepped back. And where was the music coming from?

With a sigh, Garrett dug his cell phone out of his pocket. Oh—his ringtone.

"Hey, Mom." He ran his hand through his hair, pushing it away from his face. "Sorry, I didn't mean to worry you. I stopped to see Jenna's store." He nodded. "Sure. I'll ask her. See you in a bit."

He stuffed the phone back in his pocket and caught her gaze again. "She wants you to join us for supper."

"I can't do that. Your whole family will think we're…"

"They won't think anything. I told them after we reconnected at the concert, we became friends. Come with me. My folks always loved you."

And Jenna loved them. She'd once expected them to be her in-laws. But every time she'd seen them since the breakup, it had been awkward and she hated that. Visiting them with Garrett would be even more awkward.

"I'm not hungry anyway. Tell her thanks for the offer, but I had a big lunch."

"You're sure I can't convince you."

If she kept looking into his beckoning green eyes, she'd do whatever he wanted. She straightened a pillow on the shelf. "I'm sure."

But she wasn't sure of anything. Not since Garrett's concert.

"Think about the video."

"I will." She'd dreamed the video. Over and over.

"Let me at least walk you to your car."

"I'm parked out back in the alley."

"I'll have my driver come around there."

"That's not necessary." She double-checked the lock on the front door. "I've left after dark countless times."

"I distinctly remember Mom telling me about some stalker harassing a business owner here last year."

"That was actually Caitlyn. But it turned out he'd been married to her aunt who'd been missing for thirty years and he thought Caitlyn was her. Long story."

"Sounds like, but I'd prefer walking you out."

She sighed. "Tell your driver to turn between the Hall of Fame and the Hyatt Place Hotel."

"Maybe I can convince you to do the video on the way."

That was what worried her.

Lord, I need every bit of strength You can send my way.

The brick street of the Fort Worth Stockyards in front of the Texas Cowboy Hall of Fame was strangely still. Fort Worth officers and Fort Worth Herd drovers lined each side on horseback as Garrett's limo driver stopped. He tucked his ponytail down the back of his shirt and lowered his cowboy hat as he exited the limo.

Two security men flanked him and drew attention. The last thing he needed was some overzealous fan spotting him.

But his disguise seemed to work.

Should he salute the officers or something? He waved before entering.

The lobby stirred with guests. Was Jenna here yet?

"Mr. Steele." A museum employee greeted him, warm and professional. "I'll show you to your table."

His security detail faded into the background as he followed his escort.

The museum floor had been cleared of the wagon display. Round cloth-covered tables with programs and settings lined the space while folks milled about wearing cowboy hats and Western attire from casual to formal. His tuxedo jacket and dark jeans fit right in.

Inductees lined the front tables near the stage and he spotted Clay. Had Natalie wrangled him a seat at Jenna's table as they'd discussed?

"Here we are." His escort stopped and he scanned the faces at the round table. Lane and Natalie, Mitch and Caitlyn. And a lady with her back to him.

Jenna.

But she was between her two cousins, leaving Garrett's seat between the other men. Too far apart to speak easily. At least he'd get the chance to look at her.

She turned and her gaze met his. Her eyes widened. Beautiful in a rhinestone-spangled golden dress with Western detail.

"Garrett, you're our mystery guest?" Caitlyn's gaze went to Jenna, checking her reaction.

Natalie looked uncomfortable. A different look for his usually confident publicist. Because she felt guilty conspiring against Jenna? Because Natalie knew Jenna didn't want to be near him? Because Jenna had no feelings for him?

"Why didn't you tell me you were Clay's guest, too?" Jenna asked.

"You didn't ask. And Clay has several tables. I didn't know we'd end up at the same one." His chest twinged as the lie slipped from his lips.

"Garrett?" Sammie Sanderson, her red dress a second skin, stopped beside him. "This is a surprise."

"Good. When Clay invited me, I almost said no because I didn't want to take the spotlight off the inductees. We kept my attendance under wraps." He gestured to the place card at his seat—Mystery Guest.

"And you happened to end up at the same table as Jenna." Sammie grinned as if she knew more than she did.

"We're all high school friends." Natalie shot Sammie a *there's-no-story-here* glare. "I'm Garrett's publicist and Jenna is my cousin. And my sister Caitlyn married Clay

Warren's cousin. We're all guests of Clay's, and Jenna didn't even know who our Mystery Guest was until Garrett arrived."

Way to skirt the issue without revealing you knew, Nat.

"Listen, Sammie." Garrett took her hand in his. "If you'll do me a favor and make sure we have a peaceful evening, I promise you'll be the first to know if my love life improves."

"Promise?" Sammie went from reporter to flirty in two seconds flat.

"You have my word." He kissed the back of her hand.

"Maybe I'll see you after this shindig." Her words came out all breathy.

"Maybe." He let his gaze linger on Sammie's much longer than he wanted to.

It worked. She giggled and headed to the inductee's table.

His eyes met Jenna's cold stare.

One of the men cleared his throat. Uncomfortable tension, so thick a bowie knife couldn't cut it, settled over the table.

"What?" Garrett shrugged. "I was sidetracking her. Keeping rumors at bay and Jenna out of the spotlight."

Her gaze dropped to the centerpiece, a gold-painted cowboy boot filled with dried flowers.

Could she be jealous?

His heart warmed.

Better make small talk and not let the press catch him staring at her. "So, Mitch, Mom said you're a Texas Ranger now."

"Yep. I'm a forensics artist."

"Impressive." Garrett turned to Lane. "What are you doing these days?"

"I'm a pickup man."

"For the rodeo," Natalie added, stroking her husband's cheek. "Not women."

"Got all the woman I need." Lane stilled her hand and kissed her palm.

As the couple made eyes at each other, Garrett expected a heart to outline them. Happy. In love.

Why couldn't he have that?

Because he'd blown it with Jenna. But not this time. He had to hold on to her. "Jenna's thinking about being in my next video."

Her glare painted a bull's-eye on him.

From possibly jealous to downright livid in one second flat.

"You didn't tell me about that." Caitlyn's tone echoed surprised disbelief.

"I only learned about it yesterday. But I'm not really—"

"Natalie had this great idea." Maybe if he could get her cousins excited, Jenna would catch the enthusiasm. "She wanted me to do the infamous concert run with a Jenna look-alike actress. But I said, why not Jenna?"

"Because *Jenna* doesn't like publicity." Jenna sipped her water.

"But publicity could get you a store in the Galleria." His gaze caught hers and held.

"He's right, Jenna." Caitlyn clapped her hands. "Just think, one little ole video and your dreams could come true."

"I've already had a taste of reporters hounding me." Jenna shuddered. "I think I'll pass."

"But Garrett said he'd do an interview prevideo and explain you're doing a favor for him since y'alls concert run struck such a chord with fans." Natalie shrugged. "Really, Jenna, I was skeptical at first, but it's a win-win opportunity."

"She's thinking about it." He grinned. "I can tell. In the meantime, anybody going to my Billy Bob's concert tomorrow night?"

Everyone at the table nodded.

Except the concertgoer he wanted. She ignored him.

"Jenna, you're not going?" Natalie prodded.

"The only time I ever went to a Garrett Steele concert, it came back to bite me. Think I'll steer clear."

His heart landed in the toes of his cowboy boots.

Clay's wife, Rayna, stepped between Caitlyn and Mitch. "I'm so glad y'all came. We're so excited about Clay getting inducted."

"He deserves it. One of the greats." Lane tipped his hat.

A server set salads in front of Caitlyn and Jenna, then made his way around the rest of the table.

"Thanks. I better get to my seat." Rayna turned away.

The room quieted as the focus turned to food.

Jenna barely glanced his way again.

Curled on the cream-colored love seat in her sewing room, Jenna tucked her event program into the protective sleeve in her scrapbook. She arranged her place card bearing her name on the corner of the page above a picture of the cowboy-boot centerpiece.

Had Garrett connected with Sammie after the ceremony? Or after the Billy Bob's concert last night? Or both?

Flirting with every woman he saw. He couldn't seem to help himself. No matter who was around to watch. No matter whose heart his antics shattered.

Why was she still thinking about Garrett? She'd told her cousins she didn't want any concert details. Garrett was officially gone. Out of her life again. Wasn't that what she wanted?

Maybe she shouldn't have kept the ceremony memorabilia for her scrapbook. She flipped the album closed, then slipped it back in the shelf. It was supposed to be a reminder of her evening honoring Clay Warren and the other worthy inductees. Not a memory of Garrett.

At least the press had paid her no attention lately. But business was getting back to normal. Steady, but not hopping. Mostly ready-made cowboy couture. Fewer custom orders and even fewer elegant orders. A sea of Western designing lurked in her future.

Her shoulders slumped. Another scrapbook caught her eye. *My Dream*—spelled out in curlicue writing surrounded by roses, lace and ribbon stickers. She pulled the album and laid it on the coffee table.

Pictures of the Galleria and the space she wanted plus fabric swatches and notes of what she'd carry in her store, along with her custom-made services. The ready-made line had come to life as planned. But at the Stockyards, the line came in at the bottom of her sales.

The doorbell gonged and she hurried to peer through the peephole.

Natalie.

She swung the door open. "What are you doing here?"

"You won't believe it." Natalie did a little bounce on the balls of her feet.

"You're pregnant?"

"Not yet. But I was at the Galleria today. Guess what retail space is up for lease?"

"Oh, don't tell me." Jenna clamped her hands over her ears.

"Your dream store. Stop it." Natalie pulled her hands away. "Have you thought any more about the video?"

"No. No. No."

"This could be your chance, Jen. It's like God is lining everything up for you. All you have to do is your part."

Could this be God's plan? For her to fulfill her dream? Surely there was another way. In fact, there was. All she had to do was lay down her pride and tap into her trust fund. But she was so proud of the store she'd built on her own. Even if her top seller was branding iron curtain rods.

If she used her trust fund, would she feel as accomplished with her dream store? She couldn't do it. And she couldn't torture herself doing a video with Garrett.

"No. No. No."

"Stop saying that. Do the video, lease the store and design satin confections till your heart's content."

Her cell vibrated in her pocket. Saved by the buzz.

"I have to get this." She dug her phone out.

Garrett.

She closed her eyes.

The scrapbook. The available store. Garrett's call. Something was definitely lining up. *Is this You, Lord?*

"I thought you had to get that." Natalie elbowed her.

"It's him."

"Perfect timing—like God set it up." Natalie grinned. "Tell him you'll do the video." She grabbed at the phone. "Or I will."

Jenna evaded Nat's grasp and jabbed the talk button. "Hello."

"Hey, Jenna." His voice turned her insides into melted butter.

"Hey."

"I hoped I might see you at the concert. I even had my security guys watching for you."

"I told you I planned to steer clear."

"I was still hoping. Anyway, I called to let you know the video is all set. But the production schedule hinges on casting. Have you thought any more about it?"

"I'll do it." She squeezed her eyes shut.

Natalie let out a whoop.

"That went a lot easier than I expected. Who is this and what have you done with Jenna?"

"My dream space is available for lease at the Galleria."

"Oh." Hurt sounded in his voice.

But he was using her for publicity. Her heart tightened. Why shouldn't she return the favor?

"I'll let my production team know. We'll film at American Airlines Center, so we'll have to work around their schedule, as well. Anything important on your calendar we need to work around?"

"My schedule's pretty open."

"I'll get back with you on dates, then. And, Jenna, even though we both have ulterior motives, I look forward to working with you."

"You may live to regret it." *I know I will.* "I have no experience with making videos."

"You'll be fine, as long as you're you. The whole world will fall in love with you all over again."

But she didn't care about the whole world. She cared only about how Garrett felt about her. Why couldn't *he* fall in love with her all over again?

They said good-night and she clutched the phone to her heart. "What am I doing?"

"I'm very proud of you." Natalie laid a hand on her arm.

"What do I tell Mama?"

"Hmm." Nat nibbled her lip. "That it's the pathway to your store. That is why you're doing it, isn't it?"

Jenna's gaze locked with her cousin's. It was all there. Natalie knew. Yes, she wanted the store, but she also wanted to be with Garrett. "You being his publicist doesn't mean you don't have to keep the cousin code."

"Your secret's safe with me. Besides, it's your job to tell Garrett you're still madly in love with him. Not mine."

But *he* wasn't madly in love with *her* anymore. And even if he were, she still didn't want to tag along on his concert tours. Especially with two stores to run.

Garrett slid into his leather jacket and headed out of makeup. He still had trouble with that concept.

His voice had to hold up. He'd gotten Natalie off his back by seeing his doctor. And downplayed his doctor's stern warning to rest and let the swelling go down before further testing.

All for this. A week with Jenna.

A glimpse of her in the hall halted his feet. Dressed in her leopard-print top, black jeans and heels with straps up to her ankles, she was a blast from the Dallas concert. His heart did a giddy two-step just like when he'd caught sight of her in the lobby barely a month ago.

"That shirt brings out golden flecks in your eyes and hair. Like it was made for you." He swallowed hard. "Stunning."

"Thanks." Her cheeks pinked. "Caitlyn sold out and had to order more. Who knew its one showing would make headlines?"

A vision of her in the gold dress from the induction ceremony—onstage while he sang to her—popped into his head. He'd mention it to Nat. "Ready?"

She sucked in a big breath. "No."

"Don't be nervous. All you have to do is what you did at the concert that night. Pretend you're there again. Did you watch the footage last night?" He'd watched so many times, he knew every nuance by heart.

She nodded.

"Then you're good to go." He led her toward one of the concession windows, where a crowd milled about.

"Who are all these people?"

"Mostly extras with a few yet-to-be-discovered actors and actresses sprinkled in."

"There y'all are." A gray-haired man approached them.

"This is Roger Leon, our director."

Roger shook Jenna's hand. "We'll start in the lobby today and try to get to the stage."

"Try? That'll take, like, two minutes."

"Dear Jenna." Roger smiled. "I won't lie—filming this video in one week will be grueling. Camera angles, expressions, stumbles all come into play. You'll make your lobby run countless times. In fact, you might want to change into tennis shoes."

"I didn't bring any."

"Oh." Roger scratched his chin. "What size do you wear?"

"Seven and a half."

"We'll get you a pair."

"But I have a perfectly good pair at home. I'll make do today and wear them back tomorrow."

Garrett cleared his throat. "You won't be going home tonight."

"I won't?" She stared him down.

Chapter 7

Was Jenna onto his scheme—to do anything to spend time with her?

Garrett cleared his throat again. "Because our schedule is so tight on the video, we're all staying at the Hyatt this week. We have an entire floor." And he purposely hadn't told her because he knew she'd refuse.

"I'll go home. Each night."

"If you do that, you'll have to get up at four o'clock."

Her shoulders slumped. So not a morning person. He'd known she'd cave when she heard the early hour. Of course, staying at the hotel would only buy her two hours. But he'd share that minor detail with her later. All he wanted was every evening with her. For one week. Candlelight dinners— just talking. And winning her love.

"But I didn't even bring an overnight bag. I have to at least go home tonight and pack a suitcase."

"Make a list and I'll have someone pick up whatever you need."

"Now that that's settled, here's what I need you to do." Roger went into production mode.

Garrett disconnected from the director's instructions. A week spent with Jenna. Daily. Holding her hand. Singing to her. Could life get any better?

If only she were here because she wanted to be. Because she wanted to spend time with him. But instead, she was here only to make her dream store come true. Not his dreams.

He'd have to change that. A whole week lay before him. A whole week to lasso her heart.

Aching feet. Jenna slid her heels off inside the door of her hotel room, didn't even pause in the living room and headed straight for the bedroom. The queen-size bed cradled her tired bones. The words *cut* and *action* would echo in her dreams. A full day of filming and they hadn't even made it to the stage yet. And this video would take only a week?

Barely a month ago, she'd told herself she'd never meet him at a hotel again. Ever. Here she was staying in that same hotel with him right down the hall. For a whole week.

She could conk out right now fully dressed, makeup still on, despite Garrett's proximity.

A knock sounded at the door.

Room service? She hadn't ordered anything. She dragged herself up and her stomach growled as she hurried to the door and squinted through the peephole.

Garrett.

"I come bearing food."

"I'm not hungry." She opened the door a crack, but a wheeled cart awaited, holding plates with fancy dome covers. Her stomach growled.

The corner of his mouth twitched. "Really?"

"Okay, I'm starved. But almost too tired to eat."

"We'll make it fast." He started to push the cart into the room.

But she didn't step aside.

"I thought since we're both eating, we might as well eat together." He pulled a cover. "I assume you still like your steak medium-well."

Boy, did she. And the baked sweet potato oozed butter

with glistening steamed green beans along with a large slice of pie drizzled with pecans, caramel and fudge. Was that turtle cheesecake? Her heart hitched. He remembered all her favorites.

"If I let you in my room, what will people think?"

"The only people on this floor are my band and staff. They're not paid to think."

"I'm not comfortable with it."

"We'll pull the dining table into the living room and leave the entry door open." He waved the cover over her plate.

Steak filled her senses. "Okay." She stepped aside.

"I thought a man's stomach was the way to his heart. I'll have to remember this—it works on Jenna Wentworth, too."

No. Because Jenna Wentworth's heart was closed to Garrett Steele. It had to be. Because even if Garrett had changed, even if he was the Garrett she used to know, she could never trust him to settle in Aubrey. And be content.

And she couldn't live a life on the road—one hotel after another. Not even for Garrett.

Garrett dredged up every memory he had of when he used to pray over his meals. His words actually sounded pretty good. If only Someone were listening.

As soon as he finished, Jenna popped a bite of steak in her mouth. Her eyes closed.

"Why didn't you tell me you were hungry? We could have stopped production for a snack."

"I didn't want to mess up the schedule."

Because she didn't want to prolong this interlude with him. She was here only for her store.

"So tell me, why are you so opposed to using your trust fund for your store?"

"My mother grew up poor. She's very thrifty and Daddy wasn't rich when they married. I was a teenager when

Wentworth Commercial Real Estate finally hit it big." She mashed her sweet potato in with the puddle of butter in the middle.

"So when I graduated from design school, she challenged me to try to make it on my own and use the trust fund they'd set up for me as a safety net. That way I'd always have it in case of emergency."

"Smart woman. My dad has always counseled me to save, save, save, too."

"I doubt you have to worry about your income."

"No. But you never know." He swallowed hard. "I could wake up tomorrow and not be able to sing."

He wanted to tell her. Share his worries with the woman he loved. Instead of her cousin. But he wasn't ready to reveal his plans for his rest yet. And Jenna wasn't ready to hear it.

"I don't see that happening." She finished her meal and leaned back in her chair with a big yawn.

If only he could stay, keep her up half the night. Talking. Drowning in her beauty. But she had an early day ahead of her that she still didn't know about.

"One more thing and then I'll let you get some rest." He lifted the lid on the only remaining covered dish to reveal a pair of tennis shoes.

Her eyes widened. "Those are mine."

"Caitlyn was coming to check her Galleria store this afternoon, so Natalie called to see if you needed anything. I gave her the list you made."

"Thank you. My feet are killing me." She yawned again.

"Do you need a wake-up call?" He stood, set the shoes at her feet and pushed his cart to the door. "We're due in makeup at six."

"In the morning?" Her voice rose.

"Sorry. We can start later, but it'll take longer to shoot the video."

"No. Six is fine. I have an alarm on my phone."

"Night, then." He shot her a wink. "Dream of me."

Her sharp intake of breath echoed in his heart as he shut the door behind him. He'd certainly dream of her.

A pounding sound. Distant voice. Jenna rolled over and curled the pillow around her ears.

"Jenna." Garrett's voice. Calling to her. Not a dream.

She sat upright. Where was she? Why was Garrett pounding on the door?

The video. She squinted at the clock. Five-thirty.

"Oh, no." She threw the covers back, grabbed her robe and hurried to the door.

What must she look like? But she didn't have time to worry about it now. She flung the door open.

"Oversleep?" Garrett leaned casually against the door-frame holding her gold dress and shoes she'd worn to the Hall of Fame ceremony.

"Where did you get those? And why?"

"Caitlyn. I had an idea and Roger liked it. You're wearing this once we get to the stage."

"But I didn't wear it to the concert."

"No, but Roger thought a wardrobe change was in order and the video doesn't have to be exactly like the concert. It's a fantasy sequence to go with the song."

He was definitely her fantasy. Black leather—looking downright yummy even at such a horrid hour. And she must be a scary sight.

"I'm so sorry. I didn't even hear my alarm. Give me a minute to dress and throw on some makeup."

"Don't worry about makeup. They'll do that on-site. And don't worry about your clothes. Natalie had Caitlyn send over three more sets, so we don't have to worry about them being laundered every night. Wear your tennis shoes, bring your heels, and we'll be all set."

"At least let me brush my teeth." She scurried to the

bathroom and peered in the mirror. Oh, dear. Definite bed head with the long layers around her face standing at attention, her crown mashed flat and frizzled tendrils down her back. Pale skin with sheet lines on one cheek and dark circles under her eyes.

She brushed her teeth, calmed her hair and dressed in a pumpkin-colored button-up blouse and jeans, then took a deep breath and straightened her shoulders, before striding out to face him.

Garrett sat on the couch, holding her sandals in one hand and her tennis shoes in the other. "Ready?" He handed her the tennis shoes.

"No."

"Maybe you can nab a nap in the limo."

With him watching? Yeah, right. He'd already seen her at her worst. No way was he watching her drool.

The intensity of his eyes sent a shiver through her. If she didn't stop looking at him, she might drool even without the nap.

Galleria store. Galleria store. Galleria store.

That was why she was here. Wasn't it?

The video was almost over already. Garrett couldn't believe it. His time with Jenna had flown past and was nearing an unwanted end.

Day one, they'd made the lobby run dozens of times.

Day two, they'd made it to the stage.

Day three, Jenna had sat on the stool wearing the gold dress while he'd sung to her.

Day four, he'd sung to Jenna.

Day five, he tried not to rasp to Jenna.

The instrumental part of the song began and he knelt at her feet as she perched on the stool.

"Cut!" Roger shouted. "Look at Garrett while he's singing, Jenna."

A constant command for the past few days. She seemed to want to look anywhere but at him.

"But I didn't look at him during this part of the song at the concert and you said to do exactly what I did at the concert."

"Except for this. I need you to look at him. He's pouring his heart out to you in song—give the poor guy your attention."

She blew out a sigh and nodded.

The music started again. She looked down at Garrett. Their eyes locked and held.

"Cut!"

"What?" All of Garrett's frustration came out in his tone. Why interrupt his moment with her?

"I've got a better idea. I want y'all to dance. A two-step. A very close two-step. Circle the stage a couple of times, then when the instrumental part is over, take her back to the stool, kneel and sing the climax to her."

"I like it." Garrett grinned at Jenna.

"No." Her tone was stone cold.

"No?" Roger repeated.

"I don't dance well. And that didn't happen at the concert."

"Well, no, but the video doesn't have to be exactly like the concert."

"No." Jenna shook her head. "I have two left feet and I use them both to step on my dance partner's feet."

"That's what editing is for."

"No. I agreed to re-create the concert. We didn't dance then and I'm not dancing now."

Garrett longed to hold her in his arms. But he knew how stubborn she was and this could go on all night. Of course, that would prolong production. But she was tired. Exhausted. He didn't need to prolong her misery. That wouldn't get him anywhere with her.

And by tomorrow, he'd probably be unable to speak. Much less sing.

"Let's stick with the original plan, Roger."

"We need some sort of climax." Roger shot Jenna a scowl. "A dance. Riding off into the sunset together. A kiss." He snapped his fingers. "That's it. A kiss."

"No!" Jenna stood as if she might bolt.

"Might be fun." Garrett winked at her.

Her face pinked. "No."

"It's not like you never kissed me before," he whispered.

"That was a long time ago." She went crimson. "And I—cared about you then."

But not now. He tried not to let the hurt show.

"Eight years." He shouldn't tease her, but maybe a kiss could stir the old feelings for her. "You could refresh my memory."

"No." She took a step back from him.

"Y'all talk about it. Five-minute break." Roger dismissed the crew. "Talk her into it, Garrett."

As the stage area cleared, Jenna folded her arms across her chest. "There's no talking me into it."

"It's a video, Jenna. It doesn't mean anything."

She stiffened, her mouth tightening. "A kiss still means something to me."

Great. Now he'd hurt her by saying her kiss meant nothing. "That's not what I meant. A kiss means something to me, too." Especially her kiss. "I meant, as far as the public thinking we're an item again if we do the kiss for the video. I can downplay it in the prevideo interview I've already got scheduled."

"I'm not kissing you, Garrett. Not for the video. Or any other reason."

"What if we do a fake kiss?"

Her right eyebrow rose in a positively tantalizing way. "Fake kiss? How exactly do you do that?"

"Camera angles. All it requires is a bit of closeness." He swept her into his arms before she could evade him.

With his face pressed close to hers, he cupped her cheek in his hand. "This would look like a kiss with the right camera angle."

Her eyes locked on his. And there was something there. Something she couldn't deny. She still had feelings for him. Her gaze slipped from his and she pushed against his chest. "Let go."

The last thing he wanted to do, but Garrett released her. "Listen, Jenna, we have to give Roger some sort of climax or he'll hold this video up until we're forced to continue filming next week."

Panic dwelled in her eyes. Panic at the thought of spending more time with him. Because she cared about him?

"A dance or a fake kiss." He worked at not smiling. "And we can wrap this thing today."

"Fake kiss." She blew out a big breath and her shoulders slumped. "That'll be quicker."

Jenna's heartbeat thrummed so hard the cameramen must have heard it. Garrett knelt at her feet as the music picked up. By sheer force, her gaze met his as he sang.

Years of searching finally over,
just when I'd given up on love.
You're my lucky four-leaf clover,
only sent from up above.

Can't believe I finally found you,
I looked for you all of my life.
I don't know what I did without you,
but I know one day you'll be my wife.

The words played over and over in her heart. If only he meant them. The way he was looking at her, he could almost convince her. Almost.

List of reasons they couldn't be together. *Quick.* Even if Garrett had a trace of feelings left for her after all these years, it could never work. She couldn't traipse around the world. Not even for him. He wasn't living for the Lord. And she couldn't measure up to the women in his past. Yes, three good reasons right there. They. Could. Not. Be. Together.

As the final notes of the song faded away, Garrett stood and took her hand. Just as he'd done earlier, he pulled her into his arms.

She stiffened, but then forced herself to relax. Get it over with. His lips neared hers—a breath away—and he cupped her cheek. His eyes locked with hers and she couldn't have looked away if she'd wanted to. His lips closed in on hers.

Stay still. It's for the camera. A few more seconds and it would all be over. They'd go their separate ways. Garrett would do the interview to downplay the video. She'd still get enough publicity to open her dream store. And Garrett would begin his next tour.

His lips captured hers.

Pull away, her brain screamed. But her heart said something else. Her insides puddled and she returned his kiss. Her knees went weak and she couldn't have pulled away if she'd wanted to.

"Cut!" Roger shouted. "Let the poor girl up for air, Garrett. What happened to *fake?*"

His lips left hers and he put some space between them.

Would her legs hold her up? Her hand flew to her betraying lips. She turned her back on him and stalked away, wobbly legged.

"Wait." Roger clapped his hands. "I didn't say anything about that being a wrap."

"It's a wrap," Garrett called—close behind her. "You can fix the rest in editing."

Jenna vaulted for the stairs leading to the lobby.

"Hey, wait up." His hand closed over her wrist and he gently turned her to face him.

"You weren't supposed to kiss me." She met his gaze with a laser glare.

"I couldn't help myself." He grinned and held both palms up.

She huffed out a sigh and started to turn away again.

Both of his hands settled on her shoulders. "I'm sorry. I guess I got lost in the moment. And you didn't seem to mind." His oh-so-kissable mouth twitched with a grin.

"I was too shocked to think straight." Completely brain fried. "I'm going home. Now."

"It's late. Spend the night at the hotel as planned and leave tomorrow."

"No." She needed miles. Lots of them. Between her and Garrett's lips.

"All right. But call me when you get home so I'll know you made it okay."

"I'll be fine. And don't call me." Her voice quivered. "We're done here."

"Aren't we friends?"

"You crossed the *friends* line. And you won't get another chance."

"Jenna."

"I mean it." She raised both hands up as a shield. "Please get someone to take me back to the hotel. Do your interview. And make it believable that there's nothing going on here. Then get busy with your next tour and leave me in peace."

She started up the stairs, but three steps up, she turned. And caught him following. She jabbed a finger at him. "And. Don't. Follow. Me."

Three days since the kiss.

This time, he'd blown it—big-time. Garrett paced the

dressing room at the TV station. Shouldn't have kissed her. What man in his right mind wouldn't have? But Jenna would probably never speak to him again.

He should focus on the interview, but his thoughts dwelled firmly on the kiss. The kiss he had to downplay.

Even with his voice and career at stake, Jenna was all he could think about. If only he'd had more time with her. If only he hadn't pushed her. If only he could've had Roger stretch out the filming, but he wasn't sure how long his voice would hold out.

So where to now? Nashville. Orlando. Maybe he'd stay in Aubrey with the family instead of waiting until closer to his new nephew's appearance. And maybe he could figure out a way to spend some time with Jenna. Have her redecorate his parents' house or something. His pacing stopped.

A knock sounded at his door. "It's me," Natalie called.

He ushered her in.

"Ready? We've got about ten minutes."

"Know any real-estate agents in the area?" He leaned against the dressing table.

"My dad."

"He's commercial. I'm talking house."

"It just so happens my daughter's stepmother is in real estate. Why?" Her tone held suspicion.

"Could she be cool with me as a client? Could she keep it quiet?"

"Yes. Why?"

"I'm thinking I might unload the Orlando property. And buy a ranch in Aubrey."

"Aubrey?" Natalie propped her hands on both hips. "What are you up to, Garrett?"

"I've been thinking about taking my break near my family. And I'd rather rest at home."

"And near Jenna?"

Should have known he couldn't fool Nat. He sighed. "I

lost something eight years ago. I didn't know what I had then. But I do now. I'd like to reclaim the prize. She still has feelings for me, doesn't she?" At least, she had before he'd kissed her.

"Unspoken cousin code." Natalie shook her head. "I can't discuss Jenna's feelings with you."

Music started playing—"Does Fort Worth Ever Cross Your Mind?"

"Hang on." Natalie dug her phone out of her purse. "Natalie Gray." Silence followed.

Was it Jenna?

"Not off the top of my head, but I'll do some research. Sure. Anytime."

She hung up and slid her phone back in her bag. "Know any country singers looking for a break?"

"More than I can count."

"The Stockyards Championship Rodeo needs a new opening act next month."

"I'll get in touch with a few friends and let you know." Garrett pushed his hair away from his face, ponytailed it with one hand and let it loose behind his shoulders. "For the record, I'm still crazy about Jenna. You could tell her that if you wanted to."

"For the record, I always thought y'all were meant to be." She wagged a finger at him. "If you'll be good to her, be there for her, and not hurt her, I'll root for you. But I don't know how y'all could get past the touring issue. Jenna is dead set on living her days in Aubrey."

"You know, I thought I'd dread this forced rest. But I don't. Lately, touring is the last thing I want. I'd be happy with a lot less touring."

"That would be good for the relationship. But not for your career."

"Relationship, huh?" Garrett nudged her arm with his elbow. "She does have feelings for me."

"I didn't say that. But I didn't say she didn't, either." She rolled her eyes. "That didn't even make sense. We better get you on set."

"Made perfect sense." Garrett grinned. Natalie was as transparent as she'd always been. And apparently he was, too. But she'd confirmed Jenna still loved him.

Or at least, she had before he'd stolen that kiss.

Mama would freak out. But she'd freak out even more if she saw Garrett's interview this morning.

Jenna pulled up her address book and pushed the button.

"Hey, sweetheart. You're calling awfully early. Everything okay?"

"Um, I have to tell you something. Is Daddy there?"

"He's out riding his horse."

Good. Jenna blew out a breath. Mama could break the news to Daddy.

"You know how I was out of town last week?"

"And you were so secretive about it. As were Natalie and Caitlyn. Tell me, is it a man?"

"Not the way you think." *Just spit it out.* "Natalie and Garrett talked me into being in one of his videos."

"Garrett?" Mama's shock rang in her tone. "Video? What are you thinking?"

"Natalie says it will guarantee me business. Enough to open the Galleria store."

"But, sweetheart, you just got rid of all those reporters."

"I know. But Garrett's doing an interview this morning on *Good Morning Texas* to downplay my part in the video."

"Oh, honey, I always liked Garrett. You know that. But your lives have gone in two different directions. He's not the Garrett we knew."

But deep down he is. The same Garrett she'd loved since high school. He'd only buried a part of himself.

"I don't want you to get hurt again."

"I won't. The video is finished. We're back on our separate paths. I'm fine." It sounded good, anyway.

"Let's meet for lunch tomorrow so I can see for myself."

"Sounds good. See you then."

Jenna hung up and checked the clock. She scooped up the remote and aimed it at the TV. Then set the remote on her marbleized coffee table, scooped it up and aimed it at the TV. Again.

How could she get past Garrett, past his kiss, if she kept watching footage of him on TV? But she had to know what he said in the interview. She clicked the button and the *Good Morning Texas* theme filled her great room.

The camera panned the studio, including the set and cameramen, then zoomed in on Sammie Sanderson and Garrett seated in tall wooden director-style chairs in front of the customary window and street view behind them. As the theme song ended, the camera focused on Sammie in all her blond glory.

"Thanks for staying with us. My next guest is Aubrey's own country-music heartthrob, Garrett Steele."

The camera widened to include Garrett.

"So tell me, Garrett, you have a new project in the works?"

"I recently finished filming the video for 'One Day' and it'll debut on *Great American Country* March first."

"Ooh, I love that song," Sammie gushed. "When you recorded the song, did you expect it to become a staple at weddings?"

"I can't say I did, but it's a nice turn of events."

"So is the video set at a wedding?"

"No, my publicist got creative with it." He propped his right ankle on his left knee, looking casual and relaxed. "Since my friend Jenna Wentworth was such a sensation at my Dallas concert, my publicist thought it would be a good idea to include a Jenna look-alike in the video. But I suggested we use the real thing, and since my publicist is Jenna's cousin, she had a bit of pull."

"Jenna Wentworth is in your video?" Sammie's eyes went wide for the camera. "But I thought there was nothing between y'all. Merely friends and all that."

Jenna's heart went into overdrive. It was all a mistake. The reporters would stalk her again. She should never have done the video.

Chapter 8

Jenna's breath hinged on his answer.

"True." Garrett remained unruffled. "Jenna and I are friends. She did the video as a favor to me."

She started breathing again.

"Can you tell me the storyline for the video?"

"It's basically our Dallas concert footage with a few twists."

The kiss had been some twist all right. Her insides quivered at the memory.

"Twists?"

"Let's just say that in this case—art doesn't imitate life. In the video—I get the girl."

"Really? And you're sure that doesn't bleed over into the reality?"

"No." Garrett stared earnestly into the camera. "Jenna's opening a second interior-design store in the Galleria, plus she's busy with her Stockyards store."

What? He'd announced her store and she hadn't even checked on leasing the space yet.

"I'll soon be off on a new tour. We both have demanding schedules. In reality, since the video is done, I probably won't see Jenna again." Irony tinged his laugh. "Unless she shows up at one of my future concerts, and in the last seven years, that's only happened once."

"So less than a week away from Valentine's Day and Aubrey's most famous bachelor doesn't have a valentine."

Sammie's lips pouted even more than usual. "Any dates set for the new tour?"

"We're still putting it together."

"All right, then, you heard it here first, Texas. Garrett Steele's 'One Day' video releases March first." The camera narrowed to focus on Sammie. "I—for one—can't wait. Stay with us. After this break, Garrett will sing his number one hit for us right here."

Jenna clicked the button. The screen went blank.

Sammie was still on the prowl. At least that meant they probably hadn't connected after the Hall of Fame ceremony or the Billy Bob's concert.

Her phone rang and she scanned the ID. Natalie.

"He kissed you?"

"How did you know? That wasn't in the interview." Shock waves exploded in her stomach. She hadn't watched the entire segment. "Was it?"

"No."

Jenna started breathing again and clutched a paisley throw pillow to her unsettled abdomen.

"He asked me to call and see what you thought of the interview. Of course, I suggested he do that himself, but he enlightened me that you weren't speaking to him. I told him you could've sued him for sexual harassment."

"That's a thought. And to top things off, he announced my Galleria store—like it's a done deal. I planned to wait until the video released and see if business spiked."

"And by then, it's highly possible your dream space might not be available. I'm not crazy about his tactics, but Garrett's trying to help you out. Jump on it. Get thee to the Galleria and lease the space."

"But what if business doesn't spike?" She twisted the corner of the pillow into a tight spiral.

"It will." Natalie's voice filled with determination. "You're the concert girl and now you're the video girl. Garrett Steele plugged your business on *Good Morning Texas*. For free. You're probably already getting calls at the Stockyards store. And besides that, if business doesn't boom, it's not a sin to tap into your trust fund. You've wanted this forever, Jenna. Now's the time to go for it."

She had dreamed of it forever. She'd done the video, spent a week with Garrett and endured his kiss for this dream. It was time to pounce.

"Okay, I'll go to the Galleria this morning and I won't leave until I've leased the space."

"That's my coz. Maybe it'll get your mind off Garrett and that kiss. Which, by the way, proves what I told you."

"What's that?"

"He's still crazy about you."

"No. He's just crazy. And I'm supposed to be getting my mind off him, so please do me a favor and don't bring him up again."

No matter how much business boomed, no matter how much time and energy the new store required, she'd never forget Garrett's kiss.

For tonight, an employee break room at the hospital served as a private waiting room while the Steele family awaited the arrival of their newest addition. Even though Garrett had worn his customary ponytail tucked in his collar, ball cap and sunglasses, a teenager in the waiting area had recognized him. And chaos had erupted.

"I'm sorry."

"You already said that, son." Dad patted his shoulder. "It's not your fault."

"And it's much more peaceful here." Mom stood and paced. "But shouldn't we be hearing something?"

"Relax, dear. These things take time." Dad stopped her pacing with a hug.

"I'm anxious to hear something about our first grand-child. Finally. I was beginning to think we'd never have any."

If Mom only knew how many women could've presented her with his child. He shuddered. How had he gone so far astray?

If his life had gone as planned, he and Jenna would be married, possibly with children by now. It could've been him in there with Jenna, coaching her through the birth of their child.

The doors burst open and a teary-eyed Bradley stepped into the room.

Garrett's heart sank. "Are they okay?"

"They're both fine. He's here. Brian Garrett Steele."

A hard lump formed in Garrett's throat. "I'm honored."

"Come see."

Bradley led them to the maternity ward and into a room.

Missy looked exhausted, but the smile on her face car-ried double wattage as she gazed down at the blue bundle in her arms. A red, wrinkled face peered from the blan-ket framed by tufts of dark hair. The most beautiful thing Garrett had ever seen.

"This could be you and Jenna, bro," Bradley whispered. "Go after her. And don't give up this time."

His breath hitched.

As Mom cooed at the baby, Missy reluctantly handed him over.

"This is some Valentine's gift." Garrett slid his finger into the baby's tiny fist. "He'll be a little heartbreaker for sure."

"One Day" interrupted the peaceful room. He dug his cell out. Natalie.

"Sorry, I need to take this. I'll only be a minute." Gar-rett retraced his steps to the break room. Still abandoned, thank goodness.

"Hey. What's going on?"

"Star—the real-estate agent I told you about—she found a ranch. It's huge. Maybe too huge. Five houses, several barns and even covered arenas. The main house has five bedrooms and three baths."

Perfect. "I'll take it."

"Without even looking at it? You can't do that. What if you hate it?"

"I know a great decorator."

"So that's what you're up to."

"Not a word."

Natalie sighed. "If Jenna finds out I knew, she'll kill me."

"She won't find out from me."

"I'll hold you to it. So, when can you meet with Star to see the property?"

"Give me a couple of days. My nephew just came into the world."

"Why didn't you tell me? I'll call you in a few days with some appointment times. And give Bradley my congrats."

"Thanks, Nat."

He hung up and headed back to Missy's room. Everything was falling into place. Now, if Jenna would fall for his scheme. And in the end, fall for him.

Jenna clutched the phone to her ear, but her mind wandered as the manager mentioned other bids.

Three weeks since she'd finished the video. Since she'd seen Garrett. When would she stop measuring time by him?

"Miss Wentworth, are you there?"

"Yes, I'm sorry. I was checking my schedule."

"When can start?"

Relief coursed through her as she realized she'd gotten the bid. A new project to sidetrack her Garrett-obsessed brain.

"I'll get back with you in a few days on that. Thank you and I look forward to working with you." She hung up the phone and shouted, "Yes!"

"What have you got to be so happy about?" Tori looked as if she'd sucked on a lemon.

In fact, she'd looked that way all week.

"We got the contract to redecorate Hyatt Place."

"Awesome." No trace of excitement in Tori's voice.

"Is something wrong?"

"I think—" Tori covered her face with both hands "—I'm pregnant."

Jenna blinked. Swallowed hard. "Um, have you seen a doctor?"

"No. But I'm late."

"Home test?"

"No. I'm too scared."

"Okay." Jenna drew in a big breath. "I'll go with you— to buy it and stick around while you take it."

"Would you? Really?"

"Of course."

Tori's eyes got shiny. "Don't you want to know who the father is?"

Dying to. It had been too long for it to be Rick. Unless they'd seen each other since the concert. Had there been someone else since then? "I figure that's your business. But have you told him?"

"No." Tori shook her head and hugged herself. "He's long gone. Aren't you going to preach me a sermon?"

"No. But I might invite you to church. Seems like you still owe me a visit."

Tori rolled her eyes.

Oh, Lord, use this to scare some sense into Tori. To set her straight and turn her to You. Especially if she's pregnant. She'll need You.

A huge yawn escaped Garrett. Staying with his brother was great. But he wasn't getting any sleep with the new baby. How did Missy do it?

"One Day" started up and Garrett took his cell phone out of his pocket. *Jenna.*

He couldn't miss one word she had to say, so he stepped out on the back patio in case the baby started up. "Hey."

"I just hand-held Tori through a pregnancy test." Anger seethed in her tone.

"I can assure you I had nothing to do with that."

"I know that. But your friend Rick did."

"Rick?"

"Seems they got together again after the New Year's concert."

Garrett pinched the bridge of his nose. "I'm sorry to hear that. So is she? Pregnant?"

"No."

"Thank goodness. She doesn't seem to have it together enough to be a single parent and Rick certainly wouldn't be any help."

"Tell Rick if he's gonna cheat—" she huffed out a sigh "—he should be a bit more careful."

"I'm really sorry, Jenna."

"It's not your fault. And I shouldn't have called you. I needed to vent."

"Vent on me anytime."

She blew out a shaky breath. "So what are you up to these days?"

"Spoiling my nephew."

"I heard. Tell Bradley and Missy congrats."

"I will. How about you? What are you up to?"

"The store's booming, I leased the Galleria space, and I got the contract to redecorate Hyatt Place at the Stock-yards."

Garrett whistled. "That's awesome. I'm proud of you."

"I doubt any of it would have happened without you."

"Yes, it would have. You're a great decorator. It might have taken more time, but it would have happened."

"I appreciate your plugs."

"I appreciate your appearance in my video. Anticipation for the release pushed 'One Day' to platinum status."

"I'm glad. It's a great song."

Written about the woman he hoped to meet someday. The one who would replace Jenna in his heart. But she didn't exist. He'd met the woman he wanted to marry long ago.

"I need to go. I don't think Tori has slept in a week. She's conked out on my couch and I don't want to wake her."

He cleared his throat. "I'll pass your message on to Rick."

"Please do. It's hard to pray for somebody I'm so mad at." Her laugh came out derisive. "But it's hard to stay mad at someone if you pray for them. So, I'll pray for him."

"Pray for me, too." His heart squeezed.

"I already do. Goodbye, Garrett."

Jenna prayed for him? Somehow, that knowledge touched the depths of his soul. And the truth stared him down—he missed God.

Marbleized floors, matching columns and elegant lighting. Perfect. Jenna spun a circle in the middle of her dream.

Row upon row of chic fabric swatches lined one wall. With her custom-designed accent pieces, artwork and ready-made lines, the store burst with sophistication.

Tomorrow March dawned. Grand-opening day and the best part—business had boomed at the Fort Worth store with mostly custom orders. She'd paid the lease on the new store without tapping into her trust fund.

"It's beautiful, sweetheart." Mama squeezed her elbow.

"Thanks. And thank y'all for all your help."

Caitlyn and Natalie buzzed about the store along with her new employees and Tori, adjusting tasteful displays.

"Your store opens the same day as the video. We couldn't

ask for better timing." Natalie set a black lamp with a damask shade near a matching pillow.

Jenna's heart tripped. She hadn't told Mama about the kiss and it hit the airwaves tomorrow along with a pickup-truck-load of publicity.

"Mama, I have to tell you something."

"What, dear?"

"About the video…"

"It was just for the video." Natalie jumped in.

"What was just for the video?" Mama's left eyebrow quirked.

"Garrett kissed her." Natalie's tone was all matter-of-fact.

"Kissed her?" Mama squeaked.

"He kissed you?" Caitlyn's and Tori's surprise blended.

"For the video." Jenna concentrated on arranging a gold silk table scarf under a matching lamp. "The director wanted some kind of climax at the end. Either a dance or a kiss. The dance would have pushed into another day of production. The kiss was quicker and I wanted to get it over with."

Why was she protecting him? It was a stolen kiss. But the truth would cause more questions and she didn't want to think about the kiss. Or Garrett. Much less talk about the kiss or him.

"Oh, Jenna, this is such a mistake." Mama paced. "All the big romance stuff will start up again. The reporters will hound you."

"I don't think so." Natalie shook her head. "Garrett handled that aspect in his *Good Morning Texas* interview. He explained Jenna did the video as a favor. I think the only publicity to come out of this will be good. Great for the new store. The timing is perfect."

"You're the marketing guru." Mama sighed. "I hope you're right."

"Besides, Garrett is gone. Who knows where? I doubt I'll see him again." Did they hear the regret in her voice?

"Didn't you ask Bradley about him when you got your taxes done?"

"Missy had their baby, so I didn't see Bradley this year."

"Wait a minute." Tori's jaw dropped. "Your accountant is Garrett's accountant?"

"Probably." Jenna grinned. "Since they're brothers."

"Why did I never know that?" Tori tossed a throw pillow at her. "And I can't believe you didn't tell me about the kiss."

"Well, you've got the scoop now. Shhh." Jenna pressed a finger to her lips.

If only she could quiet the erratic beat of her heart inspired by mere thoughts of Garrett's kiss.

Garrett paced the white-tiled floors of the main-house entryway. White walls and stone fireplace. Everything was white. A clean palette. The Rolling J Ranch—it had a nice ring to it.

"The main house is only five years old. The living room is quite large and set apart." Star, the real-estate agent, was all business—no starstruck female in sight. "As we continue into the great room, kitchen and dining area, notice the open-air floor plan."

The arched, wood-framed windows lining the back of the great room overlooked a built-in swimming pool. A tree trunk formed pillars at each end of the wall separating the great room and kitchen. A third tree joined the pillars across the ceiling and framed a long bar.

"I love the rustic look, but I don't want a bar in my house."

"The wall could be torn out, opening the kitchen to the great room. You could keep the wood and use it as a breakfast bar."

"Great idea."

"She's good." Natalie ran her hand along the bar top.

"How much acreage?"

"Three hundred fifty." Star scanned her tablet. "And there's another large house, an office with living quarters, a guesthouse, a foreman's house, three horse barns, a show barn, two covered arenas, a covered round pen, trailer storage with electricity, tractor sheds, hay barns, an eight-acre fully stocked lake and a boathouse."

"How much?"

"Twenty-two million."

"I'll take it."

"Don't you think we need to see the rest of the house at least?" Star's all-business veneer slipped as surprise sounded in her tone. "Not to mention the dozen other buildings."

"I'm game. But I'm already sold." Maybe the ranch's name was a good sign. And if everything went according to plan, he wouldn't even rename it.

"You know, for that kind of money, I could find you something you might like better. Something you wouldn't have to renovate."

He liked this woman. Not out to nab his millions, but to make sure her clients were happy.

"I appreciate the offer, but from the list of properties you gave me, this is the closest to ideal. I don't have a problem with tearing out a few walls."

Star offered her hand. "I wish all my clients were as easy to sell as you."

"I think Garrett had his mind made up before we ever got here." Natalie shook her head.

"Not a word," he whispered as they followed Star on a tour of the five bedrooms and three baths.

"Location and size are perfect." Nat lowered her voice for his ears only. "Fits right into your devious plan. This place is big enough to keep Jenna busy for months. I don't know if I can keep this from her."

"All I want is a chance to spend time with her. A chance to win her back."

"If you hurt her again—" she jabbed a finger at him "—you'll have to deal with me."

"I plan on making her the happiest woman in the world."

"That was some kiss in the video."

Some kiss indeed. Garrett grinned. He could live on the memory of it—for a while. But the memory was wearing thin.

If Jenna would fall for his plan, maybe he'd have a chance at another kiss. Not stolen this time.

Everyone had left the Galleria store for the night and Jenna did a final walk-through to make sure nothing was out of place.

Life was good. She straightened a lamp. Mere days after her grand opening and she was already in the black. If business continued to boom, she'd have to expand her factory and hire more workers.

After grand-opening week, she planned to split her time between both stores. The cowboy decor no longer grated on her nerves since her elegant line was now just as popular.

Her only problem—she missed Garrett. She hadn't heard a thing from him since she'd called to vent about Rick. And watching their video kiss over and over certainly didn't help her forget him. Pathetic.

The phone rang. After closing, but she answered anyway.

"Worthwhile Designs at the Galleria." A thrill shot through her even after getting to say that for a week.

"Could I speak to Jenna Wentworth?"

"Speaking. How may I help you?"

"This is Darrin Collins. I'm a general contractor. My

client recently bought the Rolling J Ranch and wants to hire you to redecorate."

The Rolling J? That huge, multimillion-dollar horse ranch in Aubrey with hundreds of acres, several houses and multiple barns?

If her career hadn't already been made, this would do it. "Can we meet to discuss the project?"

"Of course. When would be convenient for you?"

She checked her schedule. "How about breakfast tomorrow at Moms on Main in Aubrey?"

"Nine?"

"Yes. I'll bring a couple of my designers."

"My client requested your services to personally oversee the project. Exclusively."

"I'm not sure I can do that." She checked her commitments. "Such a large project could take months."

"My client is aware of that. I assure you, you'll be well compensated. And my client plans on hosting gatherings when the ranch is finished. Gatherings of wealthy, influential people."

"I see." Was God opening another door? "We'll discuss things over breakfast and see if we can come to an agreement."

"I'll see you then, Miss Wentworth."

"Wait." But the call ended. Who was his client?

Garrett paced the tiled floor he hated at the ranch. Now that all the walls had been taken out, construction had halted. Now completion of his project hinged on Jenna. Shouldn't Darrin be back by now?

The doorbell sounded. He was tempted to answer it himself, but it could be some random delivery person and word would get out who'd bought the place. Not only could he lose this chance with Jenna, but also his privacy.

The housekeeper stepped into the great room. "Mr. Collins to see you, sir."

"Thanks. Send him in."

Darrin stepped in the room.

"Did she sign the contract?"

"Yes."

"She agreed to exclusively oversee the project?" Garrett smiled.

"Yes. She was quite intent on learning who I'm working for."

"And?"

"I told her the paperwork was buried in a huge corporation. So deep that I don't even know who my client is."

"Excellent work. When will she be here?"

"Next week. She requested time to wrap up current projects and assign tasks to her other decorators."

"Excellent. I appreciate all your hard work. I'll be happy to give you a recommendation after you finish here."

"Thank you, Mr. Steele. I'll check with you next week." Darrin exited.

Garrett settled in the leather chair he'd bought. The only furniture in the house other than his bed. Jenna would be here next week. And she'd be livid when she saw him. Should he wait a few days before revealing himself?

That would only make her madder. And besides, he didn't want to put off seeing her any longer.

Jenna stopped her car at the closed iron gate. The terra-cotta fencing with Austin stone pillars spanned as far as she could see on each side. "This place is amazing."

"You better stay on the phone with me until you see if this person is a nut or something." Caitlyn's tone sounded leery.

"Hang on while I figure how to get inside." She pushed the button beside the gate.

"Yes," a woman answered.

"Jenna Wentworth. I'm an interior decorator. I'm supposed to meet…" Ridiculous—she didn't even know whom she was meeting. "I'm supposed to meet with someone to discuss decor."

"Yes, ma'am. We're expecting you. Drive straight ahead up the hill to the main house with the Spanish-style clay roof." The gates swung open.

"Thank you."

"Jenna?" Caitlyn's voice tugged at her.

"It's fine." Jenna pressed the phone to her ear again. "I'm driving in."

"I've always wanted to get behind those gates. What's it like?"

"So far, miles of fencing, lined by pines, with rolling hills on one side and a gigantic lake on the other." She saw the house in the distance. "I'm approaching the house now. It's white Austin stone like the fencing with a red-clay tiled roof. Definitely Spanish style."

"Don't you dare hang up."

"Relax. I've got my pepper spray." She neared the house. "And there are a dozen vehicles here. I doubt my client has plans to murder me with all these witnesses."

"I can't believe Natalie didn't think this was weird. I should have sent Mitch with you."

"I'm fine." Jenna got out of her car and approached the house. "There's a fountain with a decorative pool and courtyard. If the inside's as impressive as the outside, I'm not sure why I'm here." She rang the bell. "I just pushed the doorbell."

"Pepper spray first. Ask questions later."

The door swung open.

Garrett.

Her phone slipped from her hand and clattered on the tile.

Chapter 9

Garrett flashed a smile in hopes of charming her anger away. "You dropped something." He stooped, picked up her phone and held it toward her.

But she stood there with her hand clasped over her mouth.

"Jenna." A faint voice called over the phone. "Answer me or I'm sending Mitch over there."

"You better answer. Sounds like the Texas Rangers are gonna be on me if you don't."

She jerked her phone out of his hand and shot him a glare. "I'm fine, Caitlyn. Garrett's here. I'm assuming he's here because he's the top secret owner. On second thought, maybe you should send Mitch. If Nat knew about this, there'll be two bodies in my wake. I need to go. I've got a murder to commit." Jenna shoved the phone in her pocket, turned on her heel and marched jerky strides toward her car.

"Wait." Garrett vaulted after her. "Let me explain."

"Explain what?" She stopped and turned on him with fire in her eyes. "How you played me for a fool?"

"I wanted a place closer to my family. I fell in love with this ranch, but I hate the decor."

"You could have bought anything you wanted." Anger seethed in each word. "With all the enormous horse ranches in Aubrey, I'm sure you could have found something you liked as is. Or hired anyone else to decorate."

"Yes, but this is the only place with enough acreage to

provide complete privacy. I want to turn the office into a sound studio and open the arenas to offer roping and riding lessons. Maybe even bull-riding lessons. This place has everything I want." He spun a circle. "But inside, everything's white. An empty palette and you're the best decorator I know."

Curiosity danced in her eyes. Could she resist a peek inside the house?

"Come inside. Take a look and you'll see how badly I need your help."

"All right." She sighed. "But I'm just looking."

"It's really quite something." He pressed his hand to the small of her back to usher her inside. A jolt shot through him, the thrill of touching her.

"Wow." She stopped in the entryway and surveyed the huge white stone fireplace in the living room.

"I love the layout and the spaciousness, but it needs warmth and color." He captured her hand. "Let me show you what I've done so far."

She didn't pull away as he led her to the great room at the back of the house.

"There was a wall here." He stopped at the tree-trunk-lined bar. "But I don't want a bar, so the Realtor suggested I tear out the wall, which opened it to the kitchen, and use it as a breakfast bar."

"I love the design. I can't say I've ever seen a tree in a house."

"Me either." He grinned at the excitement in her eyes. "Think how much fun we could have in this place."

She frowned.

"I mean decorating it. Making it the showplace it should be."

"It'll take months."

"I've got time."

"What about your next tour?"

"I decided to prolong my break."

"Months of working with you." She shook her head. "I don't know."

"I promise not to be difficult." He crossed his fingers behind his back.

"You know what I mean. I'm not sure spending so much time with you is a good idea."

"Because?"

"Because my life is finally settling after the shock waves of the concert and the video."

"No one knows I bought this place. My contractor and workers signed a contract not to reveal my identity." And he held the trump card. "You signed a contract to decorate it."

"You tricked me." Her gaze narrowed.

"True." He held his hands up in surrender. "But I knew you'd never come if you knew it was me. And I'm in desperate need of your help. I'm starting to dream in shades of white. Do you have any idea how boring that is?"

A smile tugged at the corners of her mouth, but she closed her eyes. "All right. I'll do it. But only because I've never bailed on a project." Her gaze met his again. "And I won't start now."

He calmly offered his hand. "It'll be a pleasure to work with you. Again."

Her hand clasped his and electricity flared straight to his heart.

After touring the main house, Jenna sat crisscross style in the middle of the great-room floor, facing the fireplace.

"You can sit in my chair." Garrett sat on the floor across from her, leaning against the only chair in the house, hands resting on his jean-clad knees, barefoot. His hair loose.

"I'm fine." She needed to turn her back on him so she could focus. "What about the fireplaces? Are you keeping them as is? Or replacing the stone?"

"It's white, but I like the Austin stone. If we could keep it as is, but add some warmth and color with the walls and flooring. Maybe incorporate some Austin stone into a warmer-colored tile."

"Good. I need to get some ideas for what you like." She typed in *natural stone floor tile* in the search window of her laptop. "What color tile do you like?"

"I love the exterior of the house."

"So maybe various terra-cotta tones mixed with white and beige?"

"Maybe. But mix it up. I don't want boring."

"What color furnishings are you planning?"

"Brown leather. Similar to this chair."

"Okay. I recommend nothing too busy for the floor. Too much pattern might get on the nerves after a while."

"But something that's still interesting."

"A diagonal herringbone with smaller beige and white accent pieces. Maybe a ruglike pattern in the entryway with a line of pattern at the entrance of each room."

"I have no idea what herringbone is, but I'm certain it's pure genius. I knew I needed you."

Her gaze met his and her heart tripped. "Come look at this."

Garrett scooted over beside her. His knee touched hers; his hair brushed her arm. Spicy, manly, yummy cologne threatened to turn her brain to mush. This job would drive her insane.

"Maybe something like this?"

"I like that."

"Enough pattern to add interest, but not overwhelm." She closed the laptop and stood.

"You're leaving?" Garrett jumped up.

"I'll be back tomorrow with tile samples."

"Don't we need to discuss the walls? The curtains?"

"Another day. We start with the floor." She rushed out the door and bolted for her car.

As she roared down the drive, she punched in Natalie's number.

"Natalie Gray, publicist."

"You knew," she growled.

"I know a lot of things. True. But what do you think I knew?"

"You knew Garrett bought the Rolling J."

"Guilty."

"And you didn't tell me what I was stumbling into."

"I couldn't. I signed a contract as his publicist to uphold his privacy. Telling anyone he bought a ranch in Aubrey falls under that umbrella."

"I'm your cousin. And you knew he was tricking me into decorating for him. And you knew I'd have never signed that contract if I'd known Garrett was the owner."

"I didn't force you to sign the contract when you didn't know who the owner was."

Jenna sighed. "You got me there. Stupid, stupid, stupid."

"Listen, Jenna, I know it doesn't seem like it, but I'm looking out for you." Natalie's tone was persuasive. "Decorating Garrett's ranch will do wonders for your business. Movers and shakers will see your work and Garrett will be only too happy to toot your horn. And besides, you need to admit it—you're still in love with him."

"I am not." But her words fell flat.

"Yes, you are."

"But I can't."

"Relax. Decorate his house. Watch your career boom. Maybe working with Garrett will put things to rest with him. Once and for all."

Or stir things up again.

Maybe this was a mistake, but she was a decorator with not one, but two successful stores, and Garrett Steele was her client. She'd keep this professional and she'd keep her heart safely buried in a pile of swatches.

Garrett could get used to this. He circled Jenna as she sat crisscross style in the middle of his great room again.

He should probably concentrate on the tiles laid out in front of her, but that was a tough one. Even if he wasn't purposely procrastinating on every decision, all he could think about was Jenna.

Instead his gaze roamed over her slender jean-clad legs, her straight back and shoulders, the topaz-colored button-up blouse that turned her eyes the same color. If he ever found an excuse to buy her jewelry, that was what he'd get. Topaz. And diamonds.

"Hello? Do you like anything you see?"

His gaze caught hers. "Definitely."

Pink splashed her cheeks.

"I need to get the tile ordered, so you need to make a decision."

"I know." He forced himself to focus on the tile. "But this is something I'll have to live with for a long time. I want to make sure I like it."

He circled several more times. "You know, I'm thinking I might like something a bit more neutral."

"But I thought you wanted color?"

"I do. But not overwhelming."

"Maybe more of a taupe shade." She typed in something on her laptop.

"I have no idea what taupe is."

She chuckled. "Here, take a look at this."

My pleasure. Garrett settled beside her—his shoulder touching hers.

"This is taupe. It's a grayish-tan color."

"I like it. Maybe we should go with something like that."

"All right." She closed the laptop and stood. "I'll bring samples tomorrow."

"You're leaving?"

"Didn't we have this conversation already?"

Was she onto him? "Don't you need to take the samples you brought back to the store?"

"No. Just don't break them or you buy them."

"Why don't you stick around? It's a relatively warm day for mid-March. Let me show you the rest of the ranch."

Her eyes widened. "The contract didn't say anything about decorating any of the other houses."

"No, it didn't. Though I think I would like to redo them all at some point. Over time. But I'd like to show you the land and share my plan for it. We could ride. I got a new mare yesterday and she's stunning."

"I've always been curious about this place." She gazed out the row of windows lining the back of the house. "And you know I love to ride. I believe you're pulling my strings." She turned to face him.

"Is it working?"

Indecision scrolled across her expressive features. She frowned, nibbled her lip and finally smiled. "I can't resist."

If only she couldn't resist him.

"We better drive to the barn. We've got three hundred fifty acres to cover." He ushered her through the kitchen to the attached garage, then walked around his red Jeep to open the passenger door for her.

Jenna couldn't get enough air into her lungs. What was she thinking? Curiosity killed the cat. Riding in such close quarters with Garrett just might be her end.

Concentrate on the scenery. Rolling hills, wooded areas, horses grazing, the ginormous lake.

"What do you think?"

"It's beautiful."

"It is. The barns are past this hill." He topped the knoll and she could see several red roofs.

"Those are all barns? What are you going to do with all those?"

"Raise horses. And run a rodeo training school. And I'm putting a sound studio in the office, so I won't have to travel as much." He parked the Jeep near a barn, got out and came around to her side.

Raising horses was almost a given in Aubrey. The rodeo training school was intriguing, especially since Garrett had never competed in a rodeo. But the sound studio stilled her heart.

"I'm trying to talk Mom and Dad into moving into one of the houses."

"Don't they like Denton?"

"They miss small-town life. And we have to sneak around to visit each other. If they lived on the ranch, we could visit without worry." He opened her door. "That's the reason I bought this place. To be closer to my family."

"But what about your tour?"

"I could live with less touring."

"But what about your career?"

"My career." His laugh was derisive. "Don't get me wrong, I appreciate my fans, but this is never what I wanted, Jenna."

"But it is. You wanted to sing. From the time I can remember, you wanted a singing career."

"But I'm not a singer."

"You're not?" She frowned. "Could have fooled me."

He ran a hand through his hair with jerky movements. "No, I'm a glorified sex symbol. I've had six albums, countless hits, and the only awards I've been nominated for are fan voted. My demographic is completely female."

"I guess it takes time."

"No, Jenna. It doesn't take time. Usually one hit and

you're on the country-music map. But the industry doesn't see me as a serious singer."

"Garrett, you're a great singer."

"Thanks." He shrugged. "It's my own fault. I was desperate for a break. So when Desiree found me and talked me into keeping my hair and singing love songs, I jumped at the chance."

He sighed and leaned against the Jeep's fender. "And then I made a few mistakes and developed a reputation and everything snowballed from there. But for over a year, I've worked at cleaning up my lifestyle. I've lived like a monk and I'm still just a sex symbol. I don't get it. I mean—look at me."

She was. And he was mesmerizing. Lived like a monk. As in no alcohol? Or no women? Or both?

"Who has black hair, olive skin and light green eyes? It's weird and I don't see what women find so appealing."

Her hand almost shot up in the air. *I do. I do. I do.*

"Sorry." He turned toward the barn. "I didn't mean to get into all that."

"So, what are you going to do? Retire?" Her breath caught, waiting for his answer.

"I don't know. I feel like I owe people. My fans. Nat for taking me on as a client. My band. My crew." He closed his eyes. "And I still love to sing."

"Maybe you could change your image."

"I thought that's what I'd been doing for the last year or so."

"Maybe you could get a break in the Christian industry now?"

His laugh came out harsh. "I think I'd have to be on speaking terms with God to make it in the Christian industry. Besides, back when we were on speaking terms, I couldn't catch a break."

"All you have to do is speak. He's still there. Listening. Waiting to hear from you."

"Mr. Steele." A man stepped out of the barn. "I'm glad you came by today. We got the new horses in."

"Great. Thanks, Neil." Garrett patted the man on the shoulder.

And any chance she had of reminding Garrett that God hadn't forgotten him evaporated. Maybe another day.

She followed him inside the barn.

"Alabaster!" Garrett stroked a creamy palomino's jaw.

The mare nuzzled him and Garrett pressed his face against the horse's. Jenna drank in the image of true love as creature and owner got reacquainted.

"I take it she's yours?"

"I bought her two years ago from Clay Warren. She's been at Mom and Dad's until today." He rubbed his nose against the mare's silken muzzle. "I've missed you, girl. I've missed home. And lots of other things around here." His gaze snagged Jenna's.

"Here's your horse, ma'am." Neil led a matching palomino toward her.

"Thanks." Jenna took the reins and mounted the horse.

Garrett was looking way too at home here and it tugged at her heart. It looked just like the life she'd imagined with him. But he wouldn't stay. This was only an unexpected, short stop on Garrett Steele's tour. As soon as they finished the house, he'd get bored and be gone.

And she refused to be a broken heart he left in his wake.

Six barns, four houses and three hundred fifty acres later, Garrett drove Jenna back to the main residence. And she scurried away as quickly as she could while he entered the enormous white-walled house. Alone.

The day with her was great, but he hadn't meant to dump all his disappointments on her.

He sank into his lone chair. He needed to invest in more furniture, but that would only mean moving stuff around for the work crew.

The doorbell rang.

A few minutes passed and his housekeeper stepped into the room. "Mrs. Gray is here to see you."

"Thanks, Flora. Send her in."

The middle-aged woman left him alone. Efficient, strait-laced and unimpressed by him. Perfect.

"I can't believe Jenna hasn't gotten you any furniture yet." Natalie strode into the room, briefcase in hand.

"We can't get past the floor." He grinned.

"I've got the Cowtown contract." She handed him several papers.

"Great."

"Are you sure about this, Garrett? Your doctor said to rest your voice. Not sing every Friday and Saturday night at the Stockyards."

"It's two nights a week—four songs, tops. That's resting compared to my touring schedule." He stood and set the contract on the breakfast bar. "Got a pen?"

"You might want to read before you sign." She dug a ballpoint out of her briefcase.

"You read it?"

"Of course."

"And it includes everything we discussed?"

"Yes, but you don't have to sign today. Take time to read it."

"Don't need to. I trust you." He held his hand out.

"I don't understand why you want to do this." She handed him a ballpoint. "You're a huge star."

"The Stockyards is home. My first public singing appearances were opening the rodeo at Cowtown. It'll keep me on fans' minds. And I'm close to home."

"And Jenna."

"Added bonus." He autographed the signature line on the contract. "Know any good hairdressers who can handle natural curl? And can keep quiet about their clientele?"

"I'll see what I can come up with. Actually, a lady who works at Caitlyn's store in Dallas has the most unmanageable frizzy curl I've ever seen. But last week, she changed hairdressers and it was like she got a whole new head of hair. I'll find out who she uses."

"Thanks."

Natalie paused at the tiles laid out in a pattern on the floor. "Jenna's handiwork."

"Yep. I can't make up my mind. She's bringing more samples tomorrow."

"Her contract is only for three months. Better make up your mind."

"Plenty of time."

But was it? Could he win her heart in three months?

In their usual positions. Garrett sat beside Jenna on the floor, staring at tiles. Not making decisions.

The doorbell rang, but he ignored it.

"Don't you need to get that?"

"Flora will get it. It's much safer that way."

"Ahem." The housekeeper stepped into the room. "Mrs. Gray and her guest are here to see you."

He closed his eyes. "Did I have an appointment with her?"

"Your hair. Remember?"

"Oh, right. Send them in."

The housekeeper left them alone.

"Your hair?"

"Yeah, I forgot. Probably blocked it out. I need you to stay for this."

"For what?"

"Hey, Garrett… Oh, hi, Jenna." Natalie stopped in the entryway with another woman. "Did you forget our appointment?"

"I'm afraid I did."

"Sorry it's so late, but this was the only time I could manage this week," the woman said. "Would you like to reschedule?"

And Jenna looked at the woman for the first time. Tara Warren. Mitch's sister.

"Tara Warren?" Garrett smiled. "Is that little Tara Warren?"

"Not so little anymore. And it's Tara Hamilton now." Tara grinned. "Where should I set up?"

"How about at the breakfast bar?"

"Lead the way." Tara slung her oversize bag over her shoulder.

Hair. Tara was a hairstylist. Garrett must be getting his hair trimmed. Why would he want her to stay for that? "I think I'll go. You don't need me to supervise."

"Please stay." Garrett caught her hand and his eyes pleaded with her. "I need your support."

What was the big hairy deal? Why would Garrett be worried about getting his hair trimmed?

"Sorry for the setting, but I can't come to your shop." He dug a metal chair out of the closet.

"This is fine. I came prepared." Tara's tone soothed as she pulled a large mirror out of her bag and set it on the bar. "Natalie told me you're nervous about this."

"The shorter my hair is, the more it curls. And I don't like curl. That's why it's so long now. It curls less that way. But I'm trying to change my image."

Jenna's breath caught in her throat. Was he getting it cut short?

"I've got some techniques and product to help with the curl. Let's start with you showing me the length you want."

"At my chin line."

Jenna squelched a gasp.

"But anytime I've gotten it cut that length, it ends up way short, above my ears with kinky curl."

"Let's look at some styles I found online." Tara pulled a laptop out of her bag, set it on the bar and scrolled through several haircuts for men.

"There. That's how I want it." Garrett pointed to a chin-length style with slight layering and soft curl.

"I think that's doable."

"Can you really keep it from curling any more than that?"

"What I'll do is leave the layers long. That will weigh down the curl along with product and we should be able to do something similar." Tara combed through Garrett's hair. "The problem is most stylists cut hair wet. Hair shrinks when it dries and even more so if it's naturally curly."

Tara's tone soothed, but didn't patronize. "On top of that, most people pull the hair straight and cut it the length they want it, but after it dries and curls, you lose several inches of length."

"You sound like you know what you're doing."

"My best friend in high school had kinky natural curl. I got a lot of practice in on her." She caught a length of Garrett's hair between her fingers.

"Instead of pulling it straight, I'll let it fall natural and make a dry cut the length you want. Then I'll pull it straight and use that cut as a guideline. So when it curls, it'll turn out the length you want. Ready?"

Jenna's eyes stung.

"Jenna?" Natalie frowned at her. "You okay?"

"Fine, but I remember how much Garrett hated his hair in high school. This is a big deal for him."

"It'll be worth it." He shot her a grin. "Ready when you are, Tara."

Tara made the first cut. Jenna held her breath, but managed an encouraging smile. What did it mean for him to cut his hair? Could it be the start of a real change? But that change could come only when he embraced God again. She sent up a prayer.

Chapter 10

As Tara snipped, Garrett's image changed before his very eyes. With each cut, he could tell how cautious and knowl-edgeable she was and he relaxed. His gaze caught Jenna's in the mirror. She looked as if she might cry.

"Does it look bad?"

"It looks nice."

Had she liked his long hair? He'd known it didn't bother her. But he'd never thought about her being attached to it. Would she like his new look? She had to.

Yes, the change was to present a cleaner image for his career. But part of it was for Jenna.

If a toned-down look would get him back into her life, it would all be worth it. Even if his hair curled up like a poodle's.

"That's it." Tara pulled the cape off him and dusted his shoulders with a floppy, long-bristled brush. "What do you think?"

His hair was chin length, but the brushed-through curl was frizzy. "You're the first person ever to cut it the length I wanted. Ever."

"The curl's a bit frazzled, but I have a cure." She spritzed his hair with a water bottle and squirted a dab of product on her hand, then rubbed her palms together and smoothed it through his hair. "This is defrizz. It'll keep your hair from getting fuzzy. And this is gel. It'll keep your curl under con-trol." She squirted another dab of product on her hand and repeated the process. "A dime-size puddle of each product applied to damp hair. Defrizz first, then gel. Let your hair dry naturally and gently pick after it's dry. Never, ever use a blow-dryer, a comb or a brush for styling."

"You're a marvel." Garrett inspected the soft waves of his chin-length hair and turned to face Jenna. "What do y'all think?"

She bit her lip. "It looks really nice."

"Let's face it—" Natalie grinned "—there's nothing that could make Garrett Steele ugly."

"Why, thank you kindly, ma'am." Garrett shot Nat a wink. "How often should I get a trim to keep it like this?"

"Every six to eight weeks." Tara set bottles on the bar. "I brought enough product to keep your hair in top shape until then."

"And you'll make house calls?"

"If you're certain you're happy with what I've done, I'd love to." Tara did a little bounce on the balls of her feet. "Can I advertise that I cut your hair for a business boost?"

"Sure. Just don't tell them where."

"It's a deal." She offered her hand.

"Thanks." Garrett clasped her hand. "I can't tell you how relieved I am. Not a poodle in sight."

"I don't do poodles." Tara grinned. "I'll clean up and get out of your way."

"My housekeeper will take care of it."

"All right, then." Tara stashed her tools, laptop and mirror in her bag.

"This will be a definite image change." Nat flashed an approving smile. "I think you're on the right track."

"I owe you for finding me a great stylist right here in Aubrey."

"Actually, my salon's in Garland." Tara slung her bag over her shoulder.

"Did I pay you enough to cover gas?"

"More than enough." Tara nodded. "I really hope you like it. I'd hate to be the stylist known for ruining Garrett Steele's hair. You know, maybe I should wait and see what your fans think of the transformation before I admit my guilt."

The two women left them alone and Garrett turned to face Jenna.

"Tell me what you really think. Am I going to lose all my fans?"

"Definitely not. There might be a few disappointed women, the ones who have a thing for men with long hair. But I doubt you'll lose a single fan over it."

He opened the closet door, pulled out his new white cowboy hat he'd picked from Caitlyn's online store and set it in place. "Do you think this'll help me fit in the country industry better?"

"Face it, Garrett, you're a hunk. There's no way you can get around that. Cowboy hat or not."

"A hunk?" He lifted one eyebrow.

Her cheeks pinked. "Women find you attractive, no matter what you do with your hair."

"Do *you* find me attractive?" He closed the gap between them.

"I think you know the answer to that." She took a step back. "I need to get home and organized for tomorrow. We have a lot of work to do."

He grinned. At least she still found him physically appealing.

Now, if he could appeal to her heart. His stomach growled. *Oh, that's attractive.*

"Hungry?" Her mouth twitched.

"You know what I wish?"

"What's that?"

Lots of things. But only one he could say out loud. "I

wish we could go to Moms on Main and have a burger like we did in the good old days."

"You're a bit young to be talking about the good old days." She checked her watch. "I have an idea. Grab your sunglasses and hop in my car."

Jenna put it in high gear and scurried toward the front door.

"Where are we going?"

"You'll see. You might change your shirt in case any hair got down your collar." She flashed a conspiratorial smile as she shut the door behind her.

But he'd follow. Anywhere she wanted to lead.

If only Jenna could have had the foresight to invite Caitlyn and Nat to dinner before she'd said anything to Garrett. They were both busy and now she was stuck with him. Alone.

"I need to know where we're going." Garrett fidgeted in the seat beside her. "I can't go wherever I want, you know."

"Trust me." Jenna squeezed his hand, then jerked away at the electricity flare-up. "You're incognito. No one will notice you with your new look. You don't have Garrett Steele hair. And no one's ever seen Garrett Steele wear a cowboy hat. You're just another cowboy."

"True." But he didn't sound convinced.

"I wouldn't recognize you if I didn't know you. Not without really checking you out."

"So fickle. Earlier, I'm a hunk. Now you don't think I'm worthy of getting checked out."

"You know what I mean." Her face warmed.

What was she thinking? Taking Garrett anywhere? Much less to one of their old dating haunts.

She turned on Aubrey's main street.

"Are you going where I think you're going?"

"Moms on Main. Your wish is my command."

"Do you actually think no one will recognize me?" Garrett shifted in his seat.

"If they take time to really look at you—probably. But Moms closed at nine and no customers are there."

"Did you order a to-go meal?"

"No. I called while you were changing and asked a favor. They're going to serve us after hours."

"That's awesome." He caught her hand.

Against her better judgment, she turned to meet his gaze. And melted.

"Thank you."

"Not a problem. Everybody ought to get to eat out once in a while."

"I need to make it worth their while. I'll pay whatever this is costing."

"I've got it. I'm paying the cook and servers overtime rates. My bank account has consistently grown since you dragged me on that stage in Dallas. I figure I owe you a good burger."

"You have no idea what this means to me." His gaze tugged at her heart.

"Actually, I think I do. I'd go a bit stir-crazy holed up at your ranch every day. I can't imagine living without the freedom to go where you want."

"That, too. But I meant having dinner with you. At Moms."

Say something. To break the spell. "I'm not eating with you. I'm waiting in the car."

"Oh." His gaze bounced away from hers.

Okay, maybe she could have found a kinder way to break the spell. "I'm messing with you."

His face lit up again.

Set boundaries. She lifted one shoulder. "I figure business associates eat together sometimes and I'm starving."

The light in his eyes dimmed.

But she refused to let him lasso her heart. Not again. She opened her car door. "Let's go."

Heart, don't fail me now.

Business associates. Garrett's heart lodged in the tips of his cowboy boots over that one. But at least he was having dinner with her. At Moms. Where they'd had countless dates way back when. Maybe reliving some of those times could stir her heart.

Antiques lined the high shelves on the walls as they had back then—antique guitar, a doll-size baby carriage and an old metal wash bucket. Almost as if time hadn't marched on. If only he could get those lost years back.

Their young waitress was slightly giddy over him. But she brought their food without much chatter and didn't ask for an autograph. He'd leave her one with a generous tip.

After a few meals with Jenna, he'd learned she never ate without praying over her food. A few times she'd even asked him to do it. Tonight, she did it herself and he was relieved.

He raised his head as she finished and took a bite of her burger.

No blowing it with her tonight. She made him feel like his old self. As if he'd never gotten tarnished by the trappings of fame. As if he could have a normal life. And have a home again. A quiet, normal life in Aubrey. With Jenna.

"Remember that time after the Peanut Festival when I bought your pie at the auction?"

A smile tugged at her mouth and she dabbed her lips with a napkin. "We had lunch here. And then you ate three slices and got sick. Thanks for reminding me."

"It wasn't your mouthwatering pie. It was the three slices after that huge lunch that did me in."

She chuckled at the memory and softened before his eyes. It was working.

"Remember our first date?"

"At Six Flags. And you were afraid to ride any of the roller coasters. Who takes a girl to Six Flags if they're afraid of roller coasters?"

"A guy wanting to impress a girl who loves roller coasters. But realized he couldn't quite follow through. I thought I could do it."

"Have you still never ridden one?"

"No." He twined his fingers with hers and she didn't seem to notice. "I wish we could try again sometime."

Her eyes lit up. "We should take advantage of your fans not knowing about this new look. We could go to Six Flags. Or anywhere you've wanted to go for a while."

"I don't think it would work."

"Sure it would."

"Somebody always recognizes me." He shook his head. "I've tried wearing my hair in a ponytail, sunglasses and a baseball hat. Somebody always catches on and everything turns to pandemonium."

"Ahh, but we have connections. Natalie was the publicist there and she left on good terms. Maybe she could check into renting the park on a day when they're normally closed."

"You think they'd go for that?"

"If you paid them enough." She sipped her chocolate malt. "I'll make you a deal. If I can get the park rented for a day, you'll ride a roller coaster with me."

His heart tensed. "Which one?"

"The Titan." Her smile turned wicked.

"You're evil."

"Deal?"

"Deal." He squeezed her hand.

Her gaze landed on their hands as if she'd just realized they were touching. She pulled away.

"I'm ready when you are. I still have to get all my catalogs together and ready for tomorrow."

Should have eaten slower.

"You want to go to the rodeo tomorrow night?" He stood and pulled her chair.

"Huh?" Her confused gaze met his.

"The rodeo. At Cowtown. You wanna go?"

"I guess you decided your new look would fool everyone."

"Sort of. There's something there I need you to see."

"Like what?"

"It's a surprise." He wanted to catch her hand again, but as if she read his mind, she tucked her fingers in her jean pockets.

For a moment, he'd transported her back to their past. He had to get her to remember how they'd been together. How right and good. Then convince her they never should have parted, and they could be as good together now as they'd been in the past.

Then he'd somehow juggle a rekindled relationship with her while keeping what was left of his career intact.

But how?

Taupe tiles formed an intricate pattern as Jenna laid them in place at the foot of Garrett's recliner, still the only furniture in the house other than his bed.

"Every man's dream is to have a woman groveling at his feet."

She shot him a glare. Willing her hands to stay steady and not betray her anxiety at his proximity. She pulled the final tile from its wrapping, then set it in the middle of the design she'd created. Shades of taupe and white with a Texas lone star in the middle.

"It's perfect." Garrett leaned forward with his elbows on his knees.

"Really?"

"Except, I think I like the terra-cotta better. Does the star tile come in terra-cotta?"

"Actually, it does."

"Which one do you like best?"

"It doesn't matter. It's your floor."

"I could use a female perspective. I might get married someday and I don't want to have to redecorate."

Her stomach tensed as if someone had kicked her. "The terra-cotta is warmer. The taupe is easier to add other colors with because it's such a neutral tone. But in my opinion, taupe has been done to death."

"Terra-cotta it is."

"So, let me get this straight." She shook her head. "We wasted a week getting the taupe."

"Not really. Because now I'm sure I want the terra-cotta."

"Can I get that in blood?"

"Ouch."

"Most men are usually decisive or tell me what they like and let me pick. They don't waffle back and forth."

"I plan on enjoying this house for years to come. I want to be sure I'm happy with it."

Her heart soared. Years to come? But she couldn't get her hopes up. It would never last.

"Okay." She started picking up the taupe tile, careful not to break any as they clattered together. "I'll get the order in for the tile. I thought we'd make a rug pattern in the entryway with two or three of the lone-star tiles in the middle. And we might line the threshold of each room in the lone-star tile."

"Sounds good."

"Do you need to see the terra-cotta lone star before I order it?" She pulled the tile up on her laptop and turned the screen for him to see.

"Hmm. Maybe I should see it."

And blow another day. Or two or three if he changed his mind again.

"Okay, on to paint swatches." She dug the swatches out of her bag and splayed them in a fan shape.

"Whoa. Totally overwhelming."

"Let's try them with the tile."

Garrett scooted down from his chair and settled beside her, way too close. His jean-clad knee touched hers as she held the swatches close to the tile.

"These are too yellow, in my opinion." She removed several swatches.

"Agreed."

"And these are too orange." She pushed several more shades aside. "These blend with the tile."

"That's narrowing it down, but that still leaves two dozen choices." His breath fanned her arm.

"You don't want an exact match." She pulled two or three more shades and set them aside. "You want some contrast or it'll get boring. And you don't want to go too dark. You can add darker tones in your accents—area rugs, throw pillows, artwork." She pulled the darker shades and turned to face him.

His face was only inches from hers.

Jenna's breath caught. "Does that help any?"

"Maybe." He nodded, but his gaze locked on her lips.

She pushed to her feet. Quick.

But Garrett jumped up and caught her wrist. "Where are you going?"

"I've narrowed it down for you, but you'll have to choose. It's your house."

His thumb traced circles on the inside of her wrist and her pulse rocketed. "Don't we have something else to work on?"

"Pick your color and call me. I'll bring the terra-cotta

lone stars tomorrow." She pulled out of his grasp. "I'll pick the paint up and send the painters over whenever you're ready."

"I was thinking I might paint it myself."

"Why? It's not like you don't have the money to hire it done."

"No, but I enjoy painting. And I haven't done it in years."

"All right. I'll still pick the paint up for you. So, give me a call when you decide what you want."

Lost in his eyes, she tore her gaze away.

"Wait, you promised to go to the rodeo tonight."

In a moment of weakness. And she hadn't actually committed. In fact, she'd hoped he'd forget.

"Besides, I bet your rodeo-queen cousin would love seeing you there."

She really did need to support Caitlyn, especially after what she'd been through last year.

"It's almost time." He checked his watch. "Let me change clothes and we'll go. I'll drive."

His Western shirt and jeans were perfectly fine. Why was he changing?

"I don't think I'll have time to change."

"You're fine. Very fine." He shot her a wink and turned toward the hall.

Her heart did a jig. It could take a lot of things. But not Garrett Steele's flirting.

Security guards met them behind Cowtown as Garrett parked and a cowboy ushered them in the rear entrance as if they were expected. After that, he'd pointed Jenna to the arena and told her he'd catch up with her later.

Jenna rounded the stands. Natalie and her friend Kendra sat in their usual seats.

"Saved a seat for you." Nat patted the chair beside her. "Thought you might show up."

Completely confused, Jenna claimed the seat.

Rock music blared from the speakers and Nat leaned close to Jenna's ear. "He didn't give you any clue what's going on?"

"Nothing. I was trying to get him to choose paint and the next thing I know we're going to the rodeo. He's so indecisive and he changes his mind about decor more than any woman I've ever worked with."

"He told me he really likes what you've done so far."

"We haven't done anything yet. But I wouldn't put it past him to tear out all the tile once it's done and start over."

The big tractor in the center of the arena roared to life and the overhead lights dimmed as it exited the gate. A spotlight illuminated Caitlyn in a flash of red, white and blue spangles as "God Bless the U.S.A." played. She took her initial rodeo run holding the American flag.

As the song climaxed, Caitlyn's ride sped. At the closing notes, she reined her horse to the center of the arena. The spotlight illuminated her holding the flag as the announcer prayed.

At his amen, the national anthem began playing and the spotlight expanded to include a man striding across the dirt floor.

Garrett.

Chapter 11

Jenna's breath hitched. Outing his new look—cowboy hat and all. Her knees felt weak but she remained standing with her hand over her heart.

"You knew about this." She shot Natalie the look.

"I couldn't tell you." Natalie offered a guilty shrug. "Professional confidentiality and all that."

Garrett reached the center of the arena, holding a microphone.

A million questions zinged around in Jenna's head as Garrett sang. Would he reveal his identity? Was this a test to see if anyone recognized him?

Cheering and applause echoed through the arena. If they didn't recognize the new Garrett, they knew his voice, which exploded through the arena, as strong as when he'd sung the anthem at high school football games. Stronger.

As the song closed, the announcer's voice boomed over the speakers. "Ladies and gentlemen, I see you recognized our special guest, Aubrey's own Garrett Steele."

Murmuring moved through the crowd, then more applause and wolf whistles. Garrett took his hat off. With a wave and a bow, he exited the arena. The whistles turned to boos at his departure.

"Don't worry, he'll be back to sing a bit later. Garrett's gonna be with us every Friday and Saturday night for two whole months."

The arena erupted in applause.

"Two months?" Jenna turned to Natalie. "Why?"

"I'm sure he'll tell you all about it. Want to go to his dressing room? I have access."

"Let's do that."

She followed Nat toward the bull chutes and then down into the back lobby. A few doors down from the dressing rooms Caitlyn used as rodeo queen, two beefy men flanked a door.

"She's with me." Nat gestured toward her.

One of the men knocked, then inserted a key and ushered them inside.

Garrett sat on a tall stool in the center of the room. "Well?"

"Great job. As usual." Natalie applauded. "Not just anyone can sing the national anthem and do it justice, you know?"

"Jenna?"

"More than anything, I'm shocked."

"I'm gonna leave y'all alone." Natalie shuffled toward the door. "Gotta go watch my pickup man save all the bronc riders."

"Thanks, Nat."

"See you later." Natalie waved and slipped out.

"I don't understand. Why are you performing at Cowtown for two months?"

"Natalie needed someone to fill in and I suggested me."

"Why?"

"It's home. Cowtown was the first place I performed outside of church and high school." Garrett drew in a big breath as if he savored it. Manure and all. "I wanted a break from touring and time to get to know my new nephew. But I didn't want my star to fade in the meantime. Cowtown needed a singer. I needed something to keep me in the news. We both win."

"This is why you got the haircut." She pulled the rim of his hat down. "And the hat."

"Partly. I'm not sure anybody could pull off singing at Cowtown without a cowboy hat." He checked his watch. "My second set's coming up."

"I better get out of here." Before someone stumbled upon them. "I'd prefer not to make the news again."

"Nat and my security detail are the only ones who have access to me. They'll get us to the car. I can leave right after my set. Unless you want to stay."

If she had a brain, she'd ride with Nat. She stifled a yawn. "Early is good for me. I've got this difficult client who won't make a decision and he's wearing me out."

"I'll try to do better tomorrow." He shot her a grin.

And her heart tumbled.

Do not throw yourself into his arms.

Instead, she scurried out the door and hurried back to Nat's box seats.

"Interesting visit?" Nat lifted a brow.

"I don't understand."

"He wants a break without fading out of the spotlight. Him singing here will be big news and allow him time for his family. And you."

"I'm his decorator. That's all."

"Uh-huh."

As Caitlyn exited the arena with a sponsor flag, Garrett entered again and the crowd erupted into pandemonium. Music began, but Jenna couldn't identify the song because of the deafening noise.

Finally, the crowd quieted and strains of "One Day" rang clear. Great. Just what she needed to hear to keep her heart in check.

Week two—Operation: Win Jenna's Heart. Garrett made smooth strokes with the roller across the longest wall in the great room. But he'd rather stare at Jenna.

"I can't believe you picked the color so quickly," she said from behind him.

The only reason he hadn't pulled his indecisive act was because she wouldn't have come today to bring the paint. He'd have to spend more painstaking time on the next decision to make up for it. He dipped the roller in the tray and stole a glance at her. "I did another interview with Sammie this morning. Did you see it?"

"Sorry. I missed it."

"Basically an advertisement for the rodeo. Cowtown management is hoping crowds will pick up if everyone knows I'm there."

"The coliseum may not hold them all." She shouldered her purse. "You're doing a nice painting job. I'll leave you to it."

"No." He swung around to face her. "I was hoping you'd do my corners."

Her mouth twitched. "I had several men available for this job, but you said you wanted to do it yourself. So, you can do your own corners."

"How long's it been since you painted? It's very relaxing." He picked up a brush and slid it into her hand.

"I haven't painted since I was just starting out in this business. It's messy and I like what I'm wearing."

The jade-colored blouse brought out green flecks in her eyes and the brown jeans hugged her curves. "Me too. But I've got something you can wear."

"I think you can handle it." She set the brush down and turned toward the door.

"You're breaking our contract." He caught her hand.

"There's nothing in our contract about me painting."

"You're supposed to supervise the entire project. If your painters were doing the painting, would you leave them to it?"

"I'd check in now and then."

"Do you have any idea how long it'll take me to do all this painting by myself?"

Her shoulders slumped. "Oh, all right."

"I'll get you a shirt." Regretfully, he let go of her hand and set his roller in the tray. "Don't go anywhere."

He fished an old, long-sleeved shirt out of his walk-in closet and headed back to the great room. "This should do it."

"That's a perfectly good shirt."

"It's old. I haven't worn it in years." He held up the shirt to help her into it.

"I can get it."

"I can help." He helped her shrug into it. It swallowed her slight shoulders and hung almost to her knees. Too cute. And sexy. He could totally see her as his wife, wearing his shirt.

If only he could kiss her until she promised to never walk away from him again.

She turned away—interrupting his fantasy—and tackled the corners.

Hoping to speed the project along. He'd see about that.

But he couldn't stop time. The hours flew by. With her hair in a ponytail and his no longer long enough, they worked side by side. As if they were newly married and redecorating their first house together.

As the afternoon turned into evening, his elbow grazed hers and his heart thrummed a response.

"Did anybody ever tell you, you look cute with paint on your nose?" He caught her chin and gently wiped the tip of her nose with a tissue.

"Is it gone?" Her gaze locked with his.

"Not quite." He dabbed again and with each dab his face drew closer to hers.

She pulled away, took a step back. "I'll take care of it.

It's getting late and I need to get my catalogs together for you to choose your furnishings and fabric tomorrow."

"Jenna, don't leave. You can help me finish the walls."

"I'll be back tomorrow." She shrugged out of his paint-spattered shirt and handed it to him.

At least she planned to come back. At least a week's worth of painting remained. With Jenna. And then they'd get to tackle the rest of the rooms. Plenty of alone time. But not enough for a lifetime. He had to win her for a lifetime.

An entire week of painting followed as April dawned and then another week of tiling. Three men laid tile in the kitchen and dining area, their tools clattering and scraping with progress.

And Garrett couldn't think straight. But not because of renovations. Because of Jenna. If he completely focused on her, he could even forget the impending phone call.

"So, it totally doesn't matter to me if you want pre-fab furniture or something exclusive from my store, but I need to know what you have in mind." Jenna tucked her hair behind her ear and sat down on the completed great-room floor beside him. "But this sitting-on-the-floor thing has to stop."

His bare foot was almost touching hers. He couldn't get past her tantalizing perfume. A hint of citrus and something flowery. Like Jenna—sweet—but tart if you crossed her.

"Garrett? At least look at the catalog." Her elbow bumped his and his pulse quickened.

"I'm sorry. All the renovation is distracting."

A convenient distraction to blame his absent brain on.

"This is the same line as your chair." She pointed to a picture. "Do you want to order the couch and a few more chairs to go with it?"

Something ordered from her store would take longer. "No, I only bought that chair so I'd have somewhere to relax during the renovations. I want something with your touch. Something unique."

"Okay." She dumped the catalog in the pile beside her and picked up a thick book of fabric swatches. "I narrowed the selection down by bringing only the colors that will blend with or accent the tile and walls."

Perfect. This could take years.

"You'll need to pick a fabric and design." She unfolded a large laminated board showing several different styles of couches and chairs and spread it in front of him.

"One Day" began playing. He dug his cell from his pocket. Dr. Vincent. "Sorry, I need to take this." He vaulted for the front door.

Garrett paced circles around the fountain in the courtyard. With a big breath, he closed his eyes and answered. "Dr. Vincent."

"Mr. Steele. I have your tests back. I'm afraid you have a polyp on your vocal cord. I'll need to do further testing, and no matter what tests reveal, it'll have to be removed."

Garrett sank to the porch swing. "Further testing for what?"

"There's always a possibility a growth like you have could be cancerous. But it's not a given. And even if it is cancer, it's possible it hasn't spread."

"Will I sing again?" Or even live—if it was cancer. But he couldn't bring himself to ask the rest of it.

"I can't make any guarantees. Once we find out what we're dealing with, I'm recommending a doctor in Boston for the surgery. He's performed successful surgeries on several famous singers."

"Can you send me something on him?"

"Of course. I'll email you some information and references. In the meantime, we need to set up an appointment for the biopsy. Perhaps tomorrow?"

"So soon." He pushed his hair back. Nothing to ponytail.

"We need to move fast. Just in case."

"If I have the biopsy, will I be able to sing this weekend?"

"You're not supposed to be singing period. But no, after the biopsy, you'll need to rest your voice. No speaking or singing for ten days."

"I'm afraid that's not possible. I signed a contract to perform two songs at the Stockyards Championship Rodeo every Friday and Saturday through mid-May."

"Mr. Steele, I've repeatedly cautioned you to rest your voice."

Garrett chuckled, hoping to lighten the mood. "I consider two nights a week rest."

"Trust me, your vocal cords don't. And if we're dealing with cancer, there's no time to waste."

"I appreciate your advice." Garrett traced a tile with his toe.

"Mr. Steele, we need to do the biopsy, ASAP."

"I can't. It will have to wait until mid-May."

"In the next five weeks, you could further damage your voice." There was no compromise in the doctor's stern tone. "And if the polyp is cancerous, it could spread."

"I realize that, but there's nothing I can do."

"I see." The doctor sighed. "I'll set up the appointment and have my nurse call you. In the meantime, I'll pray for you, Mr. Steele."

"Thanks." Garrett's throat closed up.

He ended the call, blew out a big breath and pressed the phone against his chest. A biopsy. Something cold and hard twisted in his stomach. Cancer. Would he even get a second chance with Jenna?

Pull it together. Don't let her know anything is up. He shoved the phone back in his pocket and headed inside.

Determination dwelled in the rigid lines of her shoulders. She sat on the floor where he'd left her. Determined he'd make a decision today. Determined to finish this job so she could walk away from him.

"Leather and paisley go nice together." Jenna held the swatch against the newly tiled great-room floor, smoothing her hand over the velvety paisley in shades of rust and light green. "We could go with something like this for accent chairs and throw pillows."

Garrett stared at the swatch.

"You okay?"

"Fine."

But would he ever be fine again? More than anything, he wanted to hold her. To draw comfort from her. But he had to keep it together.

"I like paisley."

Jenna stopped at his fence and punched in the password. The iron gates slid open.

Last week's phone call had distracted Garrett, making him even more indecisive. Who had called him? A woman? Her stomach twisted.

Today, he'd make a decision if she had to choke it out of him. They were into mid-April now, and if he kept procrastinating, she couldn't finish the project by deadline. Other clients were waiting, but besides that, she needed to finish this for her sanity. And leave Garrett behind once and for all.

Sloping hills, horses grazing, the gently lapping lake, miles of tranquillity. No wonder Garrett had fallen in love with the ranch. She rounded a curve and the ranch house appeared.

Three knocks roused no one. She walked around the side of the huge house.

Garrett paced beside the pool, on the phone. She started back to the front to wait and give him privacy.

"No, Dr. Vincent, I haven't changed my mind."

Her steps faltered and her heart crashed into the wall of her chest. Doctor? Was Garrett sick? She shouldn't listen. But if Garrett was sick—she had to know. She hovered beside the house, straining to hear, and peeked around the corner.

"I understand that, but I'll see you in mid-May as planned."

Something was wrong.

"My voice is holding up and my throat is better since my tour ended." He ran a hand through his hair and it didn't take as long as it once had.

His throat. Maybe his voice needed rest.

"Yes, I'll be there." He ended the call.

"Garrett?" Her voice came out too high as she stepped out of her hiding place.

He spun around to face her.

"What was that about?"

"You heard?"

"I didn't mean to. You didn't answer the door, so I walked around. Why are you making an appointment with a doctor?"

His shoulders slumped and he turned away from her.

"Tell me." Her knees quaked as she neared him. She was getting way too involved, but she couldn't help herself. She needed to know the truth.

Chapter 12

"I started having problems with my throat midtour. It felt irritated after each performance. I was hoarse, and my range wasn't as wide." Garrett started pacing again.

Just his voice. She could deal with that. He could deal with that. He needed rest. Her insides settled.

"I called my doctor. He wanted to see me, but I figured he'd want me to cancel the tour. I couldn't let my fans down, so I finished the tour."

"Have you been to see him yet?"

"I thought it was merely strain. I thought once the tour ended, it would get better." Eyes downcast, he nodded. "I finally went in to see him last week. I have a polyp on my vocal cord. He wants to do a biopsy."

Cancer. The unspoken word stole her breath and hung between them. Jenna's vision blurred.

Garrett stopped pacing and turned to face her. She put her arms around him.

"I'm scared." He clung to her.

"Have you told your family?"

"No. I didn't want to worry them. Even if it's not cancer, I don't know if I'll sing again."

"Let's get past the biopsy first, then we'll worry about singing."

"We will?" He pulled away enough to see her.

"I can't let you face this alone."

"I was hoping you'd feel that way." His mouth smiled,

but it didn't make a dent in the fear in his eyes. "I have a confession."

"What?"

"I've been so indecisive on decor because I didn't want to be alone with this going on."

"All you had to do was tell me." She whacked his shoulder with her fist.

His gaze locked on her lips.

With everything in her, she wanted his kiss. To comfort him and drown in him. But she couldn't. Garrett had toned down his lifestyle, but he still hadn't turned back to God.

His lips dipped toward hers.

"But none of that." She pressed her fingers against his mouth.

"You sure?" he whispered against her fingertips.

And her resolve almost melted into the pool.

"Positive." She took a much-needed step back. "I'll see you through this on two conditions."

His eyebrows lifted.

"You keep your lips to yourself. And you make quick decisions on the house."

"I'll have to have surgery. Whether it's cancer or not. The specialist is in Boston. Will you go with me for the surgery?"

"If you stick with my conditions."

"Deal." He offered his hand.

"And after you get the biopsy results, you have to tell your family what's going on."

His gaze dropped to the patio, but he nodded.

She clasped his hand, but he threaded his fingers through hers and led her to two chaise lounges with thick padded seats.

"When did you get these?"

"A few days ago. Just for today, can we not decorate?"

"For weeks, all I've wanted to do is stay on schedule with this house." She squeezed his hand. "But now…"

"Can we chill by the pool? We could even swim if you want."

Swim with Garrett. Wearing swimsuits. No way. "The 'chill' part sounds nice."

"Really?" His eyes lit up. "We can move in the shade if it gets hot."

"So far, the sun feels nice." She settled in the cushy chaise, but it was no comfort. "The biopsy is set up for mid-May? That's a month away. Shouldn't you get it done sooner?"

"I can't. I have to rest my voice for ten days afterward. No speaking or singing. I can't do that since I'm contracted to sing at Cowtown every weekend."

"I'm sure they'd understand." His life might be at stake. "Does Natalie know about this?"

"She tried to talk me out of signing the contract."

"Then why did you?"

"I needed to keep my name out there. And I don't want my fans to know about my illness."

And he'd probably procrastinated. Because he was scared. For his health. And his career. So was she.

A day spent with Garrett. Worrying about his voice. And his life.

How many more days like this would he have?

Lord, please let him be okay. He has to be.

The interview with Sammie Sanderson had obviously done the trick. Jenna scanned the capacity crowd at Cowtown Coliseum.

The crowd had gone wild during Garrett's stirring rendition of the national anthem. And now it was almost time for his second set.

Thankfully over the past month, he'd stuck to his bargain. He made quick, decisive choices with everything Jenna presented him and pretty much let her make the decisions.

With the main part of the house near completion and the bedrooms and bathrooms well under way, here she sat at his final rodeo performance.

"Hey, coz." Natalie elbowed her. "You're kind of quiet tonight."

"Eventful several weeks." Jenna turned on her. "I get the professional-confidentiality stuff, but I still don't understand how you could know the man I love might have cancer and not tell me?"

Natalie jabbed a finger at her. "Wait. A. Minute. You admitted you still love him. I knew it."

"No, I…" Jenna's face heated and she shrugged. "So, what if I do?"

"I guess facing possible cancer shoves all the small stuff aside." Natalie squeezed her hand. "I hope he's okay."

"Me too." She closed her eyes. "Either way, he has to have surgery."

"Yes, but the specialist he's scheduling with has a whole list of famous clients who've made a full recovery."

"If his surgery is a success, he'll go back on tour." She crossed and uncrossed her legs. How could she sit here calmly when Garrett's biopsy was scheduled for Monday? "If it's not, he'll be miserable. And I doubt Aubrey is exciting enough for him to stay indefinitely."

"I don't know, Jenna. I've had some good talks with Garrett. I don't think his career is as important to him as it used to be. I think this cancer scare put things in perspective for him, too."

Whatever event had been going on came to an end and the arena lights dimmed. Jenna hadn't seen any of the rodeo. Garrett monopolized her thoughts. His surgery. His health. How much she loved him.

"Ladies and gentlemen," the announcer's voice boomed. "Please make welcome in his final performance here at Cowtown, our very own Aubrey-Texas-grown Garrett Steele with the debut of his new single." The crowd erupted in anticipation as Garrett entered the arena.

Soft strains of music flowed, but the crowd didn't quiet. Garrett waited. Finally, the multitude settled down.

"This is my final performance at the Stockyards." Regret echoed in his tone. "I've enjoyed this interlude and appreciate everyone for coming out. I'm leaving y'all with a new song. Stick around afterward and I'll introduce you to a good friend of mine who'll take over as the new headliner right here next weekend."

A haunting tune filled the coliseum. And Garrett began to sing.

> Sent like an angel from above, you filled all the places
>   in my heart.
> Turned my back on my only true love and chose to
>   depart.
> I thought you'd follow me as I went after my star.
> But I broke your heart and loved you from afar.
> Wasted no time getting on with your life, you didn't
>   fall for my scheme.
> Should have made you my wife. Finally realized
>   you're my elusive dream.

Tears pricked her eyes. Could it be? Had he written the lyrics for her? Was the song about them?

Haunting words of loss and love tugged at her heart. It was their story in song. It had to be.

> Years went by but chance brought us together. If only
>   you'll take me back.
> This time I want forever. You're everything I lack.

Turned my life around for you. I'm not too proud to
    plead.
Just give me a chance, baby. You're making my heart
    bleed.
I promise this time, it's not a scheme. You're my
    elusive dream.
Please let me in your life and I'll make you my wife.

"Um, Jenna." Natalie cupped her hands to Jenna's ear.
"Is it just me? Or is he singing about you?"

"I don't know."

"I'd say you just got your own personal rodeo song. And
maybe a proposal?"

She'd soon find out. Jenna stood and hurried toward his
dressing room.

A cowboy met her in the back lobby. "I'm sorry, ma'am.
No unauthorized personnel in this area."

"She's with me," Natalie said from behind her.

"Oh, I didn't see you, Mrs. Gray."

He left them alone and Jenna turned to face Nat.

"I figured you were headed here. Want to wait for him
in his dressing room?"

"Can you do that?"

"Yes, Miss Rule-Follower, I can do that." Natalie pulled
her keys out and unlocked the door.

"Do you think this is a good idea?" Jenna bit her lip.

"I think you and Garrett need to talk. About that song.
And a lot of things." Natalie ushered her inside Garrett's
dressing room and shut the door.

Jenna surveyed the room. Nothing personal. Except a
picture by the mirror. She stepped closer. It couldn't be.
But it was. A picture of them from their senior prom. With
eyes only for each other.

The door opened behind her and she spun around.

"Ma'am, how did you get in here?" a cowboy asked.

"It's okay." Garrett held his hands up. "She's authorized."

"Yes, sir." The man left them alone.

"You know, I used to wear one of these all the time, but I don't remember it being so itchy and hot." Garrett took his hat off. "What are you doing here?"

"I like the song. A lot."

"I'm glad. I wrote it for you."

"So it is about us?"

"You catch on quick." He flashed a heart-stopping grin.

"I saw the prom picture. What's going on, Garrett?"

"Seeing you again—it made me realize I never should have left you."

Her heart tripped. "But what happens when your surgery is a success and you go back on tour?"

"I'm planning a shorter tour. Just long enough for fans to realize the surgery was a success. If it's a success."

"Think positive. So the surgery is a success and you do a shorter tour. Then what?"

"I'll come back to Aubrey. Maybe get a dog."

"You honestly think you could be happy in Aubrey?"

"I know I could be ecstatic in Aubrey." He took her hand in his. "If I had you. I'd still record albums, but at my own sound studio, so I wouldn't even have to go to Nashville. And I'd only agree to short tours with lots of home time in between."

"That's what you want? A simpler life in Aubrey with less travel?"

"More than anything."

"What about God, Garrett? Where does He fit in?"

"Let me face down the cancer thing." Garrett shrugged. "One thing at a time."

Her insides shrank and she turned away from him. "I'll get a ride home with Nat."

"Jenna. Wait."

But she didn't. She ran. Away from the man she loved. A man without enough sense to let God help him stare down cancer.

Side by side, basking in the sun, dangling their feet in his pool. Jenna's hand in Garrett's. Paradise.

Except, she'd gone with him to the doctor today. He'd had the biopsy.

After last weekend, he'd been afraid she might not come with him.

Work on the house was at a standstill and that worried her. Didn't she know he couldn't care less about the house? He only wanted her near. Not because of his throat. Or cancer. He loved her.

And he was pretty sure she still had feelings for him. She'd wanted to kiss him all those weeks ago when he'd tried. He'd seen it. But she'd nipped his attempt in the bud.

But he knew what held her back now. God.

He'd love to take up with God right where he'd left off. But he couldn't approach God because he was scared. It wasn't right.

At least having her here kept his mind off the highly anticipated, yet dreaded phone call.

With her eyes closed, he took the opportunity to stare. Long lashes fanned her cheekbones. A perfectly proportioned feminine nose slightly tipped up. Soft lips. Not too puffy, not too slim. Perfect. Just right for kissing.

Something warmed in his stomach and he forced his gaze away from her mouth. Her tawny hair splayed down her back. The sun picked out golden, honeyed highlights.

Her eyes popped open.

Busted.

"What?"

"Nothing." He typed on his laptop, his new method for

communication. "I thought you were asleep. I was thinking about getting an umbrella or something, so you don't burn."

"I couldn't possibly sleep while we wait…. I was praying for you."

Something pricked at the backs of his eyes. He'd thought about praying but didn't figure God would hear him. But if anyone could get through, it was Jenna.

"This is driving me crazy. Don't they know we're in torment here? Why don't they call?"

"What if it's cancer?" he typed. "What if treatment doesn't work? What if I die?"

"Don't even think that." Her eyes got too shiny.

"Do you think God woud—" he backspaced to correct his typo "—would hear me if I prayed?"

"God hasn't forgotten you, Garrett. You're the one who forgot Him. He's still there—waiting for you to talk to Him again."

"But I can't talk." The keys clicked with each letter.

"God hears thought prayers."

"Do you think He'd hear?" His fingers flew on the keyboard. "Even though He knows I'm only turning to Him because I'm scared?"

"Think how scared the thief on the cross must have been." Her eyes got shiny. "But Jesus made him a promise."

"'Verily I say unto thee, Today shalt thou be with me in paradise.'" Garrett closed his eyes and set the laptop aside as he poured his thoughts out to God. *Lord, I'm sorry for turning away from You. I was lonely and sad and I turned to human comfort and alcohol instead of You.*

I knew right from wrong, what You wanted for my life, and I turned my back on You. Forgive me. For all the mistakes I made. For all the people I hurt. For hurting You.

Forgive me for only turning to You now out of desperation and fear. But I need You back in my life. I love You, Lord. Amen. He opened his eyes.

Tears traced down Jenna's cheeks beside him.

He took a deeper breath than he had in years as a weight lifted from his chest, and retrieved the laptop. "He heard me." He patted his chest. "I feel it."

"I'm glad." Her words came out watery. "Really glad."

"One Day" began playing. His gaze cut to the phone on the tile beside him.

"Want me to answer it?" She gave his hand a squeeze.

He blew out a sigh, grabbed the phone and turned it to let her see the caller ID. Dr. Vincent. Fear swarmed his chest as the song echoed louder.

"So. Let. Me. Answer. It." Her words came through clenched teeth. "The suspense is killing me."

Garrett handed her the phone, stood and paced beside the pool.

"Hello. This is Jenna Wentworth." She held her breath. "Yes. Mr. Steele is here with me." Her breath came out in a rush. "I'll give him the phone."

She chased him down and held the phone to his ear. "Mr. Steele is on the line."

"Mr. Steele." The nurse's tone was all business. "Your results are negative."

A soul-deep smile kidnapped his mouth and he handed the phone back to Jenna.

"Thank you," she mumbled into the phone and ended the call. "It's not cancer. Is that what that smile means?"

All his remaining tension melted. He nodded. *Thank You, Lord.* He wished he could let out a whoop.

"Thank You." She looked heavenward and flung herself at him, almost toppling them both into the pool. "You're okay."

Reveling in the feel of her, he held on for dear life.

No cancer. No treatments. No dying. Just surgery.

Surgery that could end his career. His livelihood.

"You need to thank God for the results." She pulled away from him.

He scooped up his laptop. "Already did."

Her smile reached her eyes. "Good. And I need to call your family and invite them over so you can clue them in."

"Can it wait until I can talk?"

"I guess that's a good idea." She hugged him again. "I'm so glad you're okay."

All he wanted to do was kiss her. His heart was lighter than it had been in years. But he didn't want her to think he'd reconnected with God to win her back. He'd have to give her more time. Time to fall in love with him all over again.

June 1. Garrett's surgery date.

Jenna had never been to Boston before. And so far, she'd seen only the inside of her hotel room and the hospital. She twiddled her thumbs as she sat with Garrett's family. Out of place, but Garrett had insisted she be here.

His mother, Glenda, clutched Jenna's hand. Her eyes were the same shade as Garrett's, her hair just as curly, but blond. "I'm glad you're here."

"Me too." Bradley sipped his coffee. "Garrett might never have told us about this if not for you."

His dad, Bennett, sat across from her. An older version of Garrett. Same bone structure, same olive skin tones, same inky hair color, minus the curls and length.

"At least we know it's not cancer." Bennett shook his head. "I can't believe he had a biopsy without telling us."

"He didn't want you to worry." Jenna's voice quivered.

"I'm glad you were with him for that." Glenda squeezed her hand again. "Stubborn boy."

Inwardly, Jenna cringed. Waiting for the question about her relationship with Garrett. But it didn't come.

Thank goodness. What could she say? *I love him. And*

I'm pretty sure he loves me. But he just reconnected with God and we've been so worried about the surgery and busy with the house, we haven't talked about us. I'm here to get him through this test. Then what? Finish his house and watch him recover, then leave to go on tour. Again.

"Miss Wentworth?" A nurse stepped into the private waiting room. "Mr. Steele would like to see you. And then everyone else before he goes into surgery."

Would her legs support her? She stood and followed the nurse down a long corridor to a private operating room.

Garrett lay in the bed with monitors surrounding him.

"Hey." He reached for her hand.

"Hey. You okay?"

"I wanted to tell you something."

"What?"

"I love you."

Her heart did a little dance and her vision blurred. "I love you, too."

"I brought you to Boston and we didn't even tour the city." He cupped her cheek in his hand, catching a tear with his thumb.

"The least of my concerns."

"Maybe we can come back."

"Maybe. When you're well." She kissed his temple. "I'll send your family in now."

Halfway back to the waiting room, her legs turned to noodles. Now, if they could get past this surgery, maybe they could sort through their future. If they had one. Together. Or apart.

Garrett sat on his new couch, exclusively designed by Jenna Wentworth, and watched her scurry about, putting the finishing touches on the house. He'd obediently picked paint, flooring and furnishings for the bedrooms and bathrooms.

The doctor said the surgery went perfectly. Now it was time to rest his voice completely and wait. A few days shy of a month left on Jenna's contract to complete the house. A month of him not speaking or singing. Using only his laptop to communicate.

Now that he had things settled with God, he wanted to settle things with Jenna. But he wouldn't discuss their future by typing it. He wanted to say it.

"Hey." She returned from the living room and flipped the radio on. "Listen to this."

"Elusive Dream" played.

"I didn't know you'd recorded it."

"I ordered all my equipment and set it up in the sound studio." Thank goodness he'd aced typing in high school. "At least if my career is over, I'll go out with a new song."

"Don't think like that." She wagged a finger at him. "It's the beginning of a new album you'll complete once you're all recovered." She knelt beside him and squeezed his hand. "So Caitlyn and Mitch are getting married next month. If your doctor releases you to sing by then, she asked if you'd sing 'One Day' at their wedding."

"It depends."

"On how you feel?"

"I'll do it," he typed. "If you'll be my date."

"I think that can be arranged." Her smile warmed his soul.

Maybe they could reclaim their long-ago love. The love that had refused to die. No matter how hard he'd tried to kill it.

July blazed outside with heat waves rolling off the limo, but the air-conditioned interior made her shiver. Garrett had shown her how to adjust the temp, but she couldn't focus.

Slowly going insane behind the doctor's office. The nurse

had ushered her there, promising Garrett would be right out. *Please, Lord. Don't let it be bad news.*

His security guards appeared first, then Garrett. The two men flanked him as they rushed the waiting car. Garrett crawled in beside her and the door shut. Darkened windows surrounded them as the limo started moving.

"Well? What did he say?"

"I love you, Jenna Wentworth."

Chapter 13

"I love you." Her insides melted and she traced his jaw with her fingertips. "Hey, you can talk."

"I can do a lot of things." He pulled her into his arms.

She closed the gap between them and kissed him. With all the fervor she'd dreamed of. He pulled her closer until she couldn't breathe, then gently pushed her away.

"Didn't I try to kiss you a few months ago and you didn't let me. Now you're kissing me. I guess you were waiting to hear me say, 'I love you.'"

"The sweetest words I ever heard. But your recommitment to Christ sealed my heart."

"If you expect me to wait until our wedding night—" his gaze held hers "—you better not kiss me like that again. Just so you know, this isn't an official proposal. I'll wait till I'm fully recovered and do something really romantic."

Her breath caught.

"We'll get married and settle in Aubrey." He caught her hand as if that was all he could trust himself to touch. "And my touring schedule will be light. Only a few months at a time and maybe you can go with me some. Like an extended honeymoon. In between very short tours, I'll be home for several months. How does that sound?"

"Like a dream come true."

"Until then, we'll need to make sure some carpenters or ranch hands are around so I can remain a gentleman."

God had fixed everything. Garrett's heart. His throat. His dreams. Their dreams.

Cameramen repositioned equipment in the studio while Sammie Sanderson primped next to Garrett. Jenna stood at the edge of all the activity and gave him two thumbs up. And his heart soared.

God had been so good to him. And Garrett needed to let the world in on his blessings.

He'd gone to church with his family yesterday. And Jenna. For the first time in years. Most of the people knew him there, but the pastor had warned the newcomers before he arrived. And the congregation focused on Christ and not Garrett.

"We're live in five, four, three, two..." the director counted down.

The theme from *Good Morning Texas* played. As the song faded, the camera zoomed in on Sammie.

"We're live with Garrett Steele this morning to learn about some recent health issues he's had. Tell our viewers all about it, Garrett."

"Midtour, I began having voice problems." Garrett stared into the camera. "But I was stubborn and didn't go to the doctor when I should have."

"Because you were afraid he'd cancel your tour, right?"

"Yes. So I completed the tour and pushed the new tour back to rest my voice."

"But you did a two-month stint at the Fort Worth Stockyards Championship Rodeo."

"Against my doctor's advice." Garrett shot the camera a sheepish grin. "When I finally visited the doctor, I learned I had a polyp on my vocal cord. He did a biopsy and the growth wasn't cancerous."

"But the polyp had to be surgically removed, right?"

"A month ago, I had successful surgery and my singing voice is improving daily."

"So you'll be scheduling the new tour soon?"

"As soon as my doctor releases me, I'll let you know."

"Any other new developments in your life you'd like to share with our viewers?"

Garrett's gaze sought Jenna's. "Something very important. I was raised in church and became a Christian at a young age. But after I went to Nashville, I fell away from my beliefs. Facing biopsy results and this surgery put things in perspective for me. I've repaired my relationship with Jesus and plan on living for Him in the future."

"Uh, that's nice." Sammie cleared her throat. "Tell us about the next album. Will you build on the success of your new single, 'Elusive Dream'?"

"Yes, I'm planning a new album. 'Elusive Dream' will be the cornerstone for it."

"Well, that's all the time we have. Thank you, Garrett, for being with us this morning. So glad to hear about your amazing recovery." Sammie focused on a different camera. "You heard it here first on *Good Morning Texas*."

The theme song started up.

"And that's a wrap," the director shouted.

"This is live television, Garrett. You could have warned me about the God stuff."

"If I had, you probably wouldn't have given me the chance to say anything."

"True," she huffed. "Too late now."

One of the crew unwired him and he strode toward Jenna.

"I'm so proud of you."

"I figured it was time the world knew I'm different. And why."

"Thousands will hear about Jesus through you." She blushed. "If we weren't in a crowded studio, I'd kiss you."

"Let's get out of here, then." He tucked her hand in the crook of his arm and headed for the exit.

With Jenna by his side. Right where she belonged.

As his security guys shuffled them into a waiting car, his phone rang. He dug it out of his pocket. Mike Parish—an exec from the record company.

"Mike, what's up?"

"Saw the interview this morning. I'd like to schedule a meeting with you."

"Sure. When?"

"How about Thursday? Say, one o'clock?"

"I'll be there. Thanks." He ended the call and put his arm around Jenna's shoulders. "I've got a meeting in Nashville with my record company. Probably to discuss the new album and tour. Want to come with me?"

She leaned her head into his shoulder. "I have a new client waiting."

"I won't be gone long." Regret filled his tone. He kissed the top of her head. "I might take time to check in with Sebastian and Amanda, but I'll only be gone twenty-four hours, tops."

"You'll be gone longer once the new tour starts up."

"But not as long as before. We'll get through it."

Already their careers pulled them apart.

"You'll be back for Caitlyn's wedding, right?" She snuggled against him.

"Wouldn't miss it."

He couldn't lose her again. He wouldn't.

Garrett flipped through a magazine in the lobby of Down Home Records. He'd spent hours practicing in the sound studio but hadn't let anyone hear yet. Not even Jenna. His throat felt better than it had in months. His voice wasn't quite there yet but improved every day, and his doctor expected a full recovery.

But was he ready to record? Ready for another tour?

His heart wasn't ready to be away from Jenna.

The secretary's phone buzzed and she answered. "Yes, I'll send him in." She hung up and turned to Garrett. "Mr. Parish will see you now. This way."

With as much nonchalance as he could manage, he stood and followed the secretary. She pecked on a door and ushered him inside.

The huge cherry desk dwarfed Mike Parish. Platinum and gold records lined every available wall space.

"Garrett, have a seat." With a grim expression, Mike gestured toward the nailhead chair facing his massive desk.

Something twisted in Garrett's gut. "Mike, good to see you."

"We discussed your outing your surgery since the doctor's checkup went well. But we didn't discuss that thing you threw in at the end."

"My Christianity? That's what this is about?"

"Over the past few years, you've cleaned up your image. A few months ago, you got a new publicist. Now—" Mike thrust his hand toward Garrett "—this haircut. I signed a sex symbol turned rebel. And ended up with a tame, nice guy."

Garrett's mouth went dry. "'One Day' was number one. At the top of the charts for three weeks when it released and went platinum. And the video brought it back to number one for another month. 'Elusive Dream' is number one, and my sales barely leveled off while I've been out of the public eye. Now that the surgery is over, I'll—"

"I don't think your voice is up for the intensive touring I'd planned. Your hair won't grow fast enough and your new publicist tells me you want to shorten your next tour."

"Yes, sir." Garrett cleared his throat. "My touring has left me little time for a personal life."

"Your personal life doesn't sell records. At least, not anymore." Mike leaned back in his chair and propped his feet on his desk. "Are you aware that your contract is up for renewal?"

Garrett's breath sputtered. "With everything I've had going on—no, I hadn't thought about it."

"I've enjoyed launching your career, Garrett, but I'm sorry—the studio has decided not to renew your contract. We don't think your new image fits our brand."

He'd given his heart and soul to Down Home Records and this was what he got in return. Garrett's heart sank. A dozen arguments came to mind. None of them would matter. He wanted to knock that snide smile off Mike's face. But he'd just gone live on television and told all of Texas he was a Christian.

Live up to it, Steele. He stood and offered his hand to Mike. "It was a pleasure working with you."

Mike frowned, as if he'd expected an argument or even a punch, but he clasped Garrett's hand. "It's nothing personal. Just business."

"I understand." Garrett headed for the exit.

A bump in the road. Maybe this was God's will. Not having a career would certainly fix his problem with Jenna. They could get married and live happily ever after.

But could he live happily ever after without singing?

Clutching her bridesmaid bouquet, Jenna focused on Garrett's expression as Caitlyn and Mitch exchanged vows. His song was next and he looked worried. Was he nervous about his voice? Was he not ready to sing yet?

But it was more than that. He'd been distracted and quiet since returning from Nashville. Every question about his trip brought evasive answers or a change of subject. Had his record company insisted on a longer tour?

All the unanswered questions spun in her brain when she should be focused on the happiest day of her cousin's life.

The rustic Ever After Chapel was gorgeous with tiny clear lights wound everywhere and miles of tulle. Each of the bride's attendants wore teal-green blingy cowgirl dresses from Caitlyn's store and the groomsmen wore matching cowboy shirts and black jeans.

"I do." Caitlyn's smile could light up Dallas. And Fort Worth, too.

The pianist began the intro for "One Day." Garrett cleared his throat and began singing. Each note resonated. Pitch perfect. Garrett lost himself in the song.

As he healed before her eyes, Jenna's vision blurred. Yes, his voice was back. Maybe even better than before. And she was happy for him.

Yet his perfect pitch would take him away from her. Again.

But this time, she'd go with him on some trips. And when she couldn't, he promised to come back to her. She had to cling to that promise.

The song ended. Caitlyn and Mitch lit the unity candle as the pastor read verses on marriage, then pronounced them husband and wife. The happy couple kissed and led the bridal party toward the fellowship hall.

Jenna hugged her cousin and the Texas Ranger she'd finally married then scanned the room as guests arrived. No Garrett. Where was he? Was she afraid fans might stalk him?

Movement to her right. Garrett ducked into a classroom. She hurried to congratulate him.

His eyes widened as she opened the door, but the strain in his expression relaxed once he realized it was her.

"Your voice—it's sensational." She hugged him. "Better than before. I couldn't believe how long you held those notes."

Nothing. He didn't say anything.

She pulled away enough to look up at him. "What's wrong? Is your throat bothering you?"

"I'm fine. We'll talk later, but I think I'll head home. If I stay, I might be a distraction. Give my congrats to Mitch and Caitlyn."

"Garrett. Tell me what's wrong. Are Sebastian and Amanda okay?"

"They're fine."

"You're leaving for the tour? Soon? And it's longer than you wanted?"

"None of the above."

"Then what?" She traced his jaw with her fingertips.

"My contract is up for renewal. I didn't even realize it with everything going on. They're not renewing it."

"What? That's crazy. 'Elusive Dream' is number one. And your voice—it's better than ever."

"I'll explain later. There is a bright side—it was in my contract that I retain rights to the songs I wrote. I'll still have royalties coming in. In the meantime, you need to get back in there and celebrate with Caitlyn. Don't worry about me. I'm fine."

But was he? She pressed her cheek against his chest. "There are other recording companies. With brains. Someone else will sign you. Especially since you still own your songs."

"Possible. But that would mean more touring than I want. At least this way—we'll be together. Living our happily ever after."

But could Garrett be happy without his successful career?

The house was perfect. The tiles were cool on Garrett's bare feet as he paced the terra-cotta with splashes of white and Texas lone stars. Jenna had captured the essence of exactly what he wanted. But now she was gone, designing someone else's house. His days without her were lonely.

More than anything, he wanted to propose and marry her. But could he, with his future up in the air? Years of royalties would still come in, but was it wise to keep the ranch? Could he implement the riding and rodeo schools he'd planned with no future recording career? The sound studio would go unused.

And what would he do with himself? He'd never had a backup plan.

The doorbell rang. Flora was already gone, but no one could get through the gate without the security code. Just in case, he peered through the peephole.

Jenna.

Heart soaring, he swung the door open. "Hey. I didn't know you were coming."

Natalie stood beside her, putting a halt to the greeting he wanted.

"Neither did I." Jenna stepped inside. "Nat has news, but she wouldn't tell me anything."

"You'll never guess—not in a bazillion years—who called me." Natalie had a definite bounce in her stride.

"The *Enquirer?*"

"No, silly. Maybe you both should sit down."

"What? Just spit it out." Jenna perched on the arm of the couch and he sank into the seat beside her.

"His Calling Records."

His insides went into orbit. "The Christian label."

"They want to sign you. They saw your interview and they think it's time to launch a new genre—Christian Country music."

Jenna let out a squeal and hugged him.

"They're waiting for your call." Nat handed him a slip of paper with a name and number on it.

"They'll want me to tour."

"I already warned them that you're wanting more home time. It sounded like they were okay with it."

"This is what you've wanted." Jenna squeezed his hand.

"The label you wanted to sign with eight years ago. What are you waiting for?"

"You're okay with this?"

"I want you happy. And I always thought you should use your talent for Jesus." She stood and dragged him to his feet. "Now, go call them."

Since her cousin was watching, he barely grazed her lips with a soft kiss. If it worked out with His Calling Records, he'd need lots of lip time with Jenna to celebrate.

Through blurry vision, Jenna watched Garrett from backstage. Eight months since she'd attended his New Year's concert right here at the American Airlines Center. And so much had changed.

Topping the list—Garrett had recommitted to Christ. His surgery was a success. They still loved each other. Garrett had a new label. He'd tour less and this was his first Christian concert.

Billed as a miniconcert, tonight was geared to let fans and potential fans know he could still sing postsurgery. But barely three months since his surgery, he wouldn't be expected to perform a regular-length concert and risk his still-recovering voice.

With his new album barely started, he'd stuck with standard hymns tonight and revealed one new Christian Country song he'd written. And since the lyrics were clean, he'd sing "One Day" and "Elusive Dream." To her. Onstage.

The intro for "One Day" began. Her cue. She stepped onstage and Garrett ushered her to a tall stool. Was it the spotlight or nerves that bathed her in a sheen of sweat? She'd never be comfortable in the spotlight, but she'd better get used to it.

Holding her hand, Garrett sang the song that initially brought them together. This time, she lost herself in his eyes, knowing he meant every word.

Eight months ago, when he'd sung the song to her, she'd been so torn. Torn between her feelings for him and knowledge that their lives and worlds could never blend. But she'd been wrong.

God had fixed everything.

The song faded into the opening strains of "Elusive Dream." Garrett had asked her to dance to both songs as he sang. But she'd thought it would be too intimate and private. She'd almost promised to dance with him at their wedding, but he hadn't mentioned marriage lately. And she certainly wouldn't pressure him. He had enough pressure without her adding to it.

Garrett sang the final words to the song and the audience went wild as the music faded. "You remember Jenna Wentworth, Dallas. Remember I told you we were only friends?" He paused. And the silence turned dramatic. "I was wrong."

"What are you doing?"

He hadn't said anything about going public with their romance.

"I'm ready for the world to know—I love Jenna Wentworth."

Whistles and catcalls echoed through the applause of the crowd and Garrett dropped to one knee. "Jenna Wentworth, will you marry me?"

Her chin trembled and she pressed her fingertips to her mouth.

The crowd began to chant. "Yes. Yes. Yes. Yes. Yes."

She threw her arms around him but movement at the front of the stage caught her attention.

A familiar-looking woman. But Jenna couldn't place her. As the woman held up a poster board, Jenna saw her stomach. A very pregnant stomach. She read the sign.

This Is Garrett Steele's Baby!

Chapter 14

Desiree. She'd promised to make Garrett pay for not hiring her back. Eight months ago.

Jenna fled backstage as security confiscated the sign and escorted Desiree to the nearest exit. Garrett turned to go after Jenna.

But Sebastian caught his arm. "Sing another song. Act like nothing's up. Finish the concert. I'll see to Jenna."

He wanted to see to her himself. But Sebastian was right. He owed it to his new label. His first Christian concert. Would his label even still want him after this debacle?

Would Jenna? His insides quaked.

Surely Jenna didn't believe Desiree's claim. She was upset. Embarrassed.

Get through one more song. Then he could comfort her. Lyrics escaped him. What song was he even supposed to have closed out with?

"Amazing Grace." That wasn't the song, but he could come up with the lyrics if he focused. And he could use a dose of God's amazing grace right now.

He whispered to his guitar player. The musician transitioned into the opening strains of the song. The band followed.

Get through this song. Help me, Jesus.

Garrett sang the song as he never had before. Clinging to each word. Needing God's strength. Needing God's blessings.

He couldn't think about whether anyone in the crowd had seen the sign. If they believed it. What his record label would think. Or do. What Jenna thought. Or would do.

God's amazing grace would see him through. Even if he lost everything. Even if he lost Jenna.

Bright September daylight spread across Jenna's living-room floor. Curled in a ball, she sat on the couch, still fully clothed.

If not for Sebastian, she'd probably be wandering the streets of Dallas. But he'd gotten her a cab and paid. His words still rang in her ears. *For what it's worth, I don't believe her.*

After she got home, the house phone rang until she turned it off. Then her cell. Surely Garrett wouldn't come to her house and lead reporters there.

Now they had a story.

And Jenna remembered where she'd seen the pregnant woman. Eight months ago. Backstage. The woman who'd pushed her way into Garrett's VIP room as Jenna was leaving to meet him for dinner.

Now she knew what had taken him so long to get to the hotel.

Nausea turned her stomach and a bitter taste rose in the back of her throat.

Her doorbell rang. Great. The reporters had come anyway. She didn't move.

"Jenna, it's Nat and Caitlyn. Let us in."

That meant the story had hit the news. Her cousins had come for support. And she needed it.

She strode to the door. They'd both pulled for her and Garrett to reunite. Surely they wouldn't smuggle him here.

"You're alone." Her voice quivered. "Just the two of you?"

"Except for two security guys Garrett sent over," Caitlyn called.

Security guys? That was why the reporters hadn't shown up.

Natalie might cross her fingers and tell a little white lie for what she thought was for Jenna's own good, but Caitlyn wouldn't.

Jenna opened the door.

"Surely you don't believe it." Natalie handed her a carton of ice cream and rushed inside. "Desiree Devine is insane. She's been calling, trying to get Garrett to hire her back for months. And she said she'd make him pay for not doing it."

"I'm so sorry." Caitlyn hugged her. "We couldn't read the sign from where we sat last night. But that horrible woman has been all over the news saying horrible things about Garrett."

She needed all the hugs she could get.

"Eight months ago, when I went to Garrett's concert with Tori, Desiree came backstage as I was leaving. Garrett had talked me into having dinner with him at his hotel." Her voice quivered. "It took a long time for him to get there. I was about to leave when he finally showed up."

"Oh, come on, Jenna." Natalie propped her hands on her hips. "Do you seriously believe Garrett had sex with her and then dinner with you?"

"I know he lived a promiscuous life." Jenna hugged herself. "And he was intimate with Desiree in the past."

"The past, Jenna. Garrett was cleaning things up even before he reconnected with you." Natalie aimed the remote and clicked the TV on.

"I don't want to hear what they're saying."

"Well, you're going to." Natalie turned the sound up. "He's doing an interview with Sammie this morning to clear things up."

"So you do know Desiree Devine?" Sammie's bland newswoman tone pierced Jenna's frayed nerves.

"Yes, I know her. I'm ashamed to say, we lived together once." Regret registered in Garrett's voice and slumped shoulders.

Regret he'd shacked up with Desiree? Or regret he'd gotten caught?

"How long ago was that?"

"Almost eight years ago. I'd been in Nashville about a year. I was singing in dives and barely making enough to pay my rent. Desiree discovered me, became my agent and launched my career. I'll always be grateful to her for that."

"And you had a relationship?"

"It lasted about six months. Until she caught me cheating on her." Garrett sighed. "I'm not proud of any of this. I lived an immoral lifestyle up until almost two years ago, when I woke up with a woman I didn't remember meeting." Garrett closed his eyes. "I stopped drinking after that and stopped sleeping around." He gazed directly into the camera. "I haven't been with anyone since." Sincerity rang through his words.

He'd told her himself he'd lived like a monk. Why had she doubted him?

"So you're saying Desiree Devine's claims—that you had sex with her after your January Dallas concert and she's carrying your child—are false."

"Desiree did manage to get backstage after that concert, but we talked—that's all. I'm willing to take a blood test to prove it. And there's no chance any woman could be pregnant with my child now or in the future. Not until Jenna and I get married. And then only Jenna will ever have a chance at conceiving my child."

Her eyes stung. He still wanted to marry her? After she'd walked out on him?

"How does Jenna feel about all of this? Did you get an answer to your proposal?"

"Jenna is embarrassed, and to me, the worst part of all of this is that she's hurt. It kind of ruined the moment and she hasn't had a chance to give me an answer."

Because she wouldn't answer when he'd called. And even with his world falling apart, he was worried about her.

Sammie turned to the camera. "You heard it here first, viewers. Garrett Steele says Desiree Devine's story is fake. And the engagement might still be on. This is a Sammie Sanderson exclus—" The TV clicked off.

"See." Natalie set the remote down.

She had to go to him. Let him know she believed him. But she'd walked out on him with the world watching. How could she make it up to him?

"Natalie, can you set me up an interview with Sammie? ASAP?"

"You—Jenna Wentworth—want to go on television?"

"No. Not really. But I have to."

"To do what?"

"To tell the world—and Garrett—I believe him. Not her."

"Good for you." Caitlyn gave her a fist bump.

Her cousin's antics got a grin out of Jenna. But the pressure in her chest didn't let up.

She'd hurt the man she loved by letting him down with her disbelief. Could she ever make it up to him?

On the set of *Good Morning Texas,* Jenna stared at the camera.

"Loosen up." Sammie patted her arm. "You're so stiff. Try to be natural."

Natural. There was nothing natural about airing the personal details of her life on television. Was this what life with Garrett would be like? Maybe. But happily ever after with Garrett would be worth any cost.

"Ready?" Sammie was way too perky. "We're almost on."

"We're live in five, four, three, two…" the director counted down.

The theme song played and Sammie smiled into the camera.

Which camera? Jenna bit her lip and chose the one Sammie was looking at.

"Jenna Wentworth, owner and head designer of Worthwhile Designs with locations at the Galleria Dallas and the Fort Worth Stockyards, is here with us this morning. Not only is Jenna a much-sought-after designer, she's also apparently the girl of Garrett Steele's dreams." Sammie's lip curled in disbelief. "So, Jenna, what's your take on Desiree Devine's claims?"

Jenna swallowed the lump in her throat. "I don't believe her." Despite her nervousness, conviction rang clear in her tone.

"You're taking Garrett's side on this matter?"

"Of course. And I'd like to give him an answer to his proposal."

Sammie's eyes lit up. "Listen up, Texas. Garrett Steele's proposal hangs in the balance."

"Yes." Jenna's voice quivered, but she looked directly into the camera. "I'll marry you, Garrett. I love you and I want to be your wife."

"And the plot thickens." Sammie turned to the camera. "You heard it here first, Texas. Jenna Wentworth is standing by her man. This is an exclusive interview with Sammie Sanderson."

Had Natalie remembered to call Garrett about the interview? Had he watched? The director's voice cut into her thoughts.

"And we're clear."

"Thank you so much, Jenna." Sammie was downright giddy. "These interviews may just launch me to prime time."

Jenna stood and walked away. One of the crew unclipped her mic pack, and as soon as she could slip away, she was out the door.

Only one viewer mattered.

Garrett sat on the floor in the middle of the great room. Where he'd sat with Jenna so many times picking paint, flooring or fabrics. The tiles were cool on his bare legs under blue jean cutoffs. He still needed the other houses redecorated. But she wouldn't come back. Even for that.

The massive oak desk she'd gotten him as a housewarming gift sat in the corner. Cowhide lined the sides and the privacy panel capped with a Texas lone star in the center.

Concentrate on the good news. His new record label had promised to stick with him until a paternity test could be taken. If he passed—and he would—he'd still have a label backing him. But none of it meant anything without Jenna.

At least he'd talked his parents into moving into the largest extra house on the property. But did he even want to stay in Aubrey if he couldn't have Jenna?

The doorbell rang. He'd let Flora get it.

Movement in the entryway. He looked up.

Jenna. He jumped from the floor and was at her side in seconds.

Her hand shook as she tucked her hair behind her ear. "I talked Flora into letting me in without being announced. I hope that's okay."

"You're here." Garrett swept her into his arms. "I can't believe you're here."

"Of course I'm here. Didn't you see the show? Natalie was supposed to tell you to watch."

"She did. But I'm so distracted, I forgot."

"I can't believe this. I go on live television to answer your proposal and you weren't watching."

"You answered?" He put enough space between them to look into her eyes.

"Yes."

His chest squeezed. "Is that the answer, or yes, you answered?"

"Yes, I answered." She grinned. "And I answered yes."

Garrett kissed her and her lips yielded to his. Heat rose through him and he forced himself to pull away. "I thought you were done with me. You wouldn't answer my calls."

"I'm sorry. I was confused."

"With just cause." He cupped her cheeks in his hands.

"But when I saw your interview with Sammie, I wondered why I ever doubted you. I'm sorry I did."

"You're here now. And I'll prove it to you. I'm having a paternity test, but not until the baby is born. It's safer for the baby that way."

"You're a good man, Garrett Steele." She closed the gap between them, pressing her face into the shelter of his chest.

"I'm trying to be the man you deserve. We should wait until after the paternity test to get married. So we won't have anything hanging over our heads."

"Why? You're not the father. There's nothing hanging over our heads."

He pulled her away from him again, enough to see her. "What did I do to deserve you?"

"I can see the tabloids now." She rolled her eyes. "Some rag will run pictures of all the models in your past. And then me. I'm just Jenna Wentworth from Aubrey, Texas. There's no way I can measure up."

"You're wrong. No other woman ever measured up to you."

"They'll say I can never keep your interest."

"Don't you understand, Jenna? You're worth so much more to me than any of those women. You're the woman I was trying to forget." He rained soft kisses across her eyes, nose and cheeks. "Their beauty was only surface deep. You're beautiful inside and out. You more than measure up. You've held my interest for almost nine years and that's never going to change."

"Stop teasing me." She grabbed him, cupping the back of his head with both hands, and pressed her lips to his.

But he couldn't stay there and keep his sanity. He pulled away and she ran her fingers through his hair.

He grabbed her wrists. "Don't."

"Why?"

"It's all stiff with product."

"I don't care. I've wanted to run my hands through your hair since I first saw you at your concert."

"Really?"

"I wish you hadn't cut it." Her fingers tangled in his hair.

"Me too. Only because I hate having to fuss with it. When it was long, it didn't take product to tame the curl. His Calling says I can grow it back."

"They're sticking with you?"

"They want me to lie low until the paternity test and finish the new album, then a debut concert followed by a three-month tour. Is that something you can live with?"

"As long as I get to live with you."

"Then we better talk wedding." He rubbed his nose against hers.

"You're not just trying to get me in your bed, are you?"

"Every night. Until death do us part."

"October first?"

"The anniversary of our first date."

Her eyes grew shiny. "You remember?"

"My heart hasn't been the same since." He took a deep

breath. "But that's only a month away. Are you sure we shouldn't wait until after…?"

"I've waited almost nine years for you, Garrett. The longer we wait, the more chance there'll be of the press getting word of it. And I don't want to wait anymore."

"On the subject of waiting—" he pulled free of her and strode across the room to the other side of the breakfast bar "—you better stay over there to be on the safe side."

Her face turned an adorable shade of pink and he fell even deeper.

To throw the press off, Jenna wasn't getting married in her own church. But that was the only disappointment on her wedding day. She waited in a classroom at Nat's church with her mom and cousins fluffing her dress.

The modest sumptuous white satin with clean, classic lines suited her perfectly as Caitlyn fastened Garrett's wedding gift—a topaz-and-diamond necklace.

"I almost forgot." Natalie set two tickets on the table. "My wedding gift."

"Tickets to Six Flags." Jenna grinned.

"You and Garrett have the park to yourselves the last Friday in October. Wish I could watch him scream like a girl when he rides his first roller coaster."

"You're awesome." Jenna hugged her.

"I try." Nat smirked.

Someone pecked on the door.

"They're ready," Daddy called.

"You look beautiful." Mama tucked a stray tendril under Jenna's veil.

"Thanks."

Nat and Caitlyn ushered her into the hall where Daddy waited. He kissed her forehead and offered his arm while Clay Warren escorted Mama to her seat.

In the lobby, Jenna peered through the windowed double

doors into the sanctuary. Recently ordained, Nat's husband, Lane, waited to perform the ceremony. The groomsmen, Bradley and Sebastian, stood beside Garrett. The man of her dreams looking positively scrumptious in a dove-gray tuxedo.

The wedding march began and her vision blurred. She blinked the moisture away as a quiet vibration started up.

"Wait." Nat dug her cell phone out. Her eyes locked with Jenna's. "I have to take this."

The call they'd been waiting for—since they'd gotten news of the baby's birth yesterday. Not that the call would change anything, but it would prove Garrett's innocence to the rest of the world.

"Publicist Natalie Gray here. Yes, he's tied up right now, but I'm authorized to receive the results. Password Rolling J. What have you got for me?" Natalie smiled. "Just as I expected. Yes, I'll make sure he knows. Thank you."

"It's over." Jenna's voice caught.

"Yes, it's over. Hang on one more minute and I'll leak the news to the press." Natalie typed a quick text message. "Now, by the time you walk the aisle, everyone will know Garrett isn't a father."

"We knew it all along, but now everyone else will know, too." Daddy patted her hand.

"How's that for a wedding present?"

"It's perfect."

Daddy had insisted on a one-on-one with Garrett after she'd accepted his proposal. Neither man had ever told her what was said, but Daddy had been Garrett's biggest fan since.

The wedding march began again.

"We better get out there or poor Garrett will think you bailed." Caitlyn nudged Natalie to start the procession.

The double doors opened, and a nervous-looking Garrett caught sight of her then visibly relaxed.

Natalie entered the sanctuary followed by Caitlyn. As the song swelled, Daddy escorted her down the aisle. Her gaze locked with Garrett's.

The aisle seemed to take an eternity, but finally she stood by his side.

"Who gives this woman to be married to this man?" Lane asked.

"Her mother and I." Daddy offered her hand to Garrett and took his seat beside Mama.

She stood on tiptoe, leaning near his ear, and whispered, "Negative. Now everyone knows the truth."

Garrett's lips grazed her cheek.

The music started. "Elusive Dream"—their Rodeo Song.

Peace registered in his gaze as he began singing to her. The deep baritone strong and pure with undying love for her.

And her alone.

* * * * *